THE SLAY'S THE THING

A Small Town Cozy Mystery

LOUISE STEVENS

Edited by: Trish Long's Blossoming Pages Author Services

Cover design: Elizabeth Mackey

Proofreading: Shasta Schafer

 Created with Vellum

With so much love and appreciation to my Leo, for the 10th time!

Publishing ten books would not have been possible without your never-ending love and support.

Chapter One

"**Y**ou are seriously overqualified for the job, Amanda. You know that, right?"

I shifted in the sticky guest seat and prayed nothing permanently bad was happening to my designer skirt. Okay. Jed Pinkus might've had a point. I was overdressed for my interview to be a part-time worker at the lone gas station/mini mart in Maple Hills, Connecticut.

"I do. But I'm making some changes in my life and moving back home for a while. I need a part-time job, and you need a part-time worker. Win-win, right?" I flashed a bright grin at Jed.

The older man took off his grease-coated baseball cap and wiped the top of his bald head. His cheeks grew ruddy. "I'm sorry, Amanda. I interviewed a kid from the high school earlier today, and he's a better fit for the job."

I was being rejected for a part-time job at Pinkus Service Station. With a deep breath, I slumped in the seat and let that humiliating reality sink in for a minute. Amanda Seldon, former VP of Human Resources for one of the largest employers in Los Angeles County, had just been rejected for a job selling junk food and lottery tickets.

"Are you okay? You've gone all pale. Can I get you some water?" Jed squinted his already small eyes at me and frowned.

"It's okay. I'm fine. Thank you for your time, Jed."

"You'll find something better suited for you real soon. I just know it."

Right. Maple Hills, population 3,126 would have lots of job opportunities for me.

"Sure I will." My lackluster tone of voice didn't even fool me, let alone Jed.

"Chin up, kiddo. Things will get better. They always do."

"Until they don't." My dad's health scare last year had taught me bad things happen to good people all the time.

"But then they get better again. Life's a roller-coaster ride. You've just got to strap in and go where it takes you."

I PULLED UP TO THE WHITE COLONIAL HOUSE MY PARENTS had called home since before I was born thirty-five years ago. I parked in front of the garage, as my parents' cars were both taking up the valuable real estate inside it. During the summer I didn't mind parking outside so much, but if I was still here in the winter, it would be a bummer. I might've lived in sunny California for over a decade, but I remembered all too well the misery of clearing the snow and ice off your frigid car.

A red SUV pulled up behind my white hybrid luxury sedan. I chuckled at my ride and the fact I'd just driven it to a service station to apply for a part-time gig as a clerk. The times have certainly changed for me.

My two childhood best friends piled out of the car. Jeremy Patterson jumped out of the passenger side and ran to me, where he clasped me in a tight bear hug. Cara Diamond popped the back of the SUV and retrieved two paper bags filled to the brim.

"Can't breathe." I wheezed.

"Sorry. I'm just so happy you're back." Jeremy said with one final squeeze.

"I'd hug you too, but of course Jeremy left me to schlep the bags." Cara bobbled one bag, and I heard the clatter of glass.

I trotted to the front door, digging in my handbag for the keys as I went. "What have you got there?"

"A little bubbly and some snacks. No offense to your mom's kitchen, but since your dad's open-heart surgery, your mom has gone all in on the healthy eating thing," Jeremy said.

"You can't really blame her. It was scary stuff." I threw open the door and stepped aside to let Cara through first.

She blew an air kiss at me as she passed by and went straight down the hall to the kitchen. Cara had grown up in the house next door to mine. We spent so much time bouncing back and forth between them we could find our way around each other's houses in the dark.

Frantic and ferocious barking greeted her as she entered the kitchen. "Please tell me The Beast is secured," she called over her shoulder.

"Fluffy is in her crate. She's a tiny shih tzu, for Pete's sake. Chill."

"A shih tzu with the soul of ten rabid rottweilers." Jeremy shuddered.

I flicked on the kitchen lights and smacked him on the shoulder as I passed by to get to my beloved dog's crate.

"She had a tough start to her life. Give her a break. She's really a sweetheart."

When I opened the crate door, Fluffy charged out barking madly and headed straight for Jeremy, where she bared her teeth and growled low in her throat.

"You're right. She's charming." Jeremy backed up as if he might bolt for the front door.

"She is." I scooped up Fluffy, nuzzled her velvety little head, and was rewarded with enthusiastic face licking and tail wagging. "See. She is a little ball of love once she gets to know you."

Cara plopped the bags on the kitchen island and looked over at Fluffy and me. "Spare us the tough start to her life. Yes, she was abandoned at the shelter because she was the runt of the litter, but you took her in as a foster, hand fed her, and showered her with love. She just doesn't like other people much."

"True, it was an epic foster fail. But really, she warmed up to my friends and neighbors in Los Angeles. Eventually. She needs to feel secure first, and she's a little protective of me."

"A little protective of you?" Jeremy snorted. "That's like saying the North Pole is a little chilly."

"Agree to disagree for now. You'll see: now we're here to stay, she will get to know you and love you. I promise." I continued to hold Fluffy and perched on a bar stool opposite the island from Cara. "What have you got there?"

She pulled a bottle of champagne out of the bag and my eyes widened as I recognized the orange label as an expensive brand.

"You moving back to Maple Hills is a celebration worthy of good champagne," Cara said.

"Glasses?" Jeremy asked.

I jerked my chin to toward a cabinet on the end. "In there. Thanks."

Cara retrieved two more bottles from the paper bag and placed them in the fridge. "They're chilled, so we can open this one right now."

"Three bottles for three people? I guess this is a celebration. Remind me again where your children are?" I asked.

"Martin has a baseball game, so my mom agreed to bring him to it and then stay and watch with Charlotte. They're going to spend the night at my parents' house afterwards, so I'm free as a bird tonight." She opened the champagne with a gentle pop and poured it into the three champagne saucers Jeremy had retrieved from the cupboard.

"And what about Mitch?" I asked.

Cara's husband, Mitch, was her college sweetheart and had relocated to Maple Hills to start his optometric practice several years ago.

"He's going to have a boy's night tonight. Poker and cigars might be involved. But as long as they're not smoking them in my house." She shrugged and passed out the bubbly.

We all clinked our wine glasses and chanted, "*Tous pour un, un pour tous!*"

'All for one, and one for all' was our traditional toast, since we'd been known as the Three Musketeers growing up.

Champagne bubbles tickled my nose as I sipped. I put my glass down on the granite island and stood. "It's such a nice afternoon, why don't we take this party out to the deck? I'm just going to bring Fluffy outside to do her business and then run upstairs and change."

Jeremy narrowed his eyes. "Thank all that's holy you're taking The Beast with you."

"Fluffy. For the one-thousandth time, her name is Fluffy." I strode out of the kitchen, still holding The Beast... er ... Fluffy, and the laughter of my friends followed me out of the room.

I might be unemployed and sleeping in my childhood bedroom, but it was good to be home.

I CHANGED OUT OF MY CHIC INTERVIEW OUTFIT AND THREW on a pair of shorts and a tee shirt, which in retrospect might have been a better choice for my meeting with Jed Pinkus than my pencil skirt and heels.

"C'mon, girl. Let's go out on the deck. You'll like that, won't you?" I patted my thigh and clicked my tongue.

Fluffy's little claws clicked on the hardwood floor of the hallway as she trotted after me. I lowered my voice. "And please be a good girl with Cara and Jeremy. They're nice people, I promise."

By the time we reached the deck, my friends had placed the open champagne bottle in a stone wine cooler, put the snacks in bowls, and sat at a round table under a forest green umbrella. I inhaled deeply of the fresh air. After over ten years in LA, I savored the clean air and scent of the pine trees and apple orchard across the pond.

Jeremy scooted his legs under the table and cast a look of terror Fluffy's way.

I rolled my eyes and flopped in the seat between them. "You do realize you're being ridiculous, right?" I reached for a pretzel, broke off a small piece, and shoved it at Jeremy. "Here. Give her this, and you'll be friends for life."

"Which, ironically, is how you became our friend for

life, Jeremy." Cara opened her whisky-colored eyes wide with feigned innocence.

"Hardy har har." Jeremy snatched the pretzel from my hand and gingerly held it down toward the deck. "Here, Beastie."

I glared at him, and he smirked and said, "I meant to say, here, Fluffy."

The tiny black and white shih tzu tentatively approached the pretzel. My friend flinched when her little black nose brushed against his hand while she sniffed the pretzel. Satisfied it wouldn't harm her, she delicately took the treat from his hand and munched happily. After she swallowed, her plumed tail waved across her back. She moved under the table and flopped down on Jeremy's feet.

"See. I told you. Friends for life."

Cara plucked a tortilla chip from a basket and dunked it in the bowl of salsa. "How did the interview go at Pinkus Service Station?"

"Not well." I sighed and took a sip of my champagne. "Jed hired a high school kid over me. It was humbling, to say the least."

"Do you really need a job right away? I mean, you're house-sitting for your parents while they're away on their cross-country journey. So you're rent free, right?" Jeremy asked as he grabbed a handful of salt and vinegar potato chips.

"I am. But I do have other expenses, like my auto and health insurance, food. I don't want to use up all my life savings, so a little income would help."

"It's great you're finally following your dream to be a writer." Cara reached over and squeezed my hand.

"After my dad's open-heart surgery, it really struck home for me our time here on earth is limited, and we shouldn't waste it. Not that I was wasting it. I mean I was good at my job, and human resources is important work, but I realized I always wanted to be an author, and that dream had gotten lost somewhere along the way."

"Your dad's surgery shook a lot of people up. My dad even joined a gym, and you know he's totally sedentary. But if it could happen to your dad, it could happen to anyone. I mean, he's always been pretty fit and healthy," Jeremy said.

"The cardiologist told him he lost the genetic lottery. With his family's history of heart disease, even though he seemed healthy, his arteries were clogging. We're lucky they caught it before he had a heart attack, and he's better than he was before the triple bypass now."

Cara pointed a tortilla chip at me. "But it made your father change his life too. He took early retirement, bought the camper, and now your parents have hit the road for the summer. Which turned out great for us, because now you can stay in their house while they're traveling."

"How did it feel quitting your job, when your career has been such a big part of your life?" Jeremy asked.

My heart raced and my palms grew damp. "Scary. Really scary. But when I went back to LA after I'd come home for dad's surgery, I tried to write at night. I was exhausted all the time. I wasn't doing my day job up to my usual standards, and I struggled with the writing in the evening. I honestly have gotten more work done on my book in the week I've been here than I did in the last several months in LA. I just wish I could find a part-time job."

"You might have noticed jobs aren't exactly growing on trees here, like the apples." Cara gestured across Orchard Pond to the unimaginatively named Maple Hills Orchard, where tidy rows of apple trees dotted the landscape. "It's why I finally gave up looking and went the stay-at-home mom route. When the kids are older, I might want to go back to my marketing work, but I'll definitely have to commute somewhere. Remember how people used to come up here from the city for the summer? Now they're moving here as year-round residents and commuting. Brutal."

The city was how locals referred to New York City, and it was a two hour drive with no traffic, and when was there ever no traffic outside Manhattan? Never, that's when.

I turned to look at Jeremy and squinted into the setting sun. "What about Eric? Does he have to drive down to the city very often?"

Jeremy's husband, Eric Hendrick, was a graphic artist who was fortunate enough to work from home most of the time.

"He's got it down to about once a month. But if he has to attend a meeting or do a presentation, then he might have to go more often. It's where he is today, which is why he didn't join our little celebration tonight. He probably won't be home until after nine."

Cara leaned forward to pull the champagne bottle out of the holder and topped off all of our glasses. "Just as well. We would've had to buy another bottle of champagne if he had been here."

"So are you guys saying to get work I'll have to commute to New York? The traveling would seriously cut into my writing time. It would be worse than when I lived in LA."

Cara raised one shoulder and let it drop. "Or Hartford. Maybe New Haven or Springfield, but there's not much here."

"Or is there?" Jeremy asked and looked pointedly from me to Cara.

"Um ... no. Some high schooler snatched the prime gas station job, so that leaves me with zero options."

"Actually I have some great news. Angie Duncan broke her leg." A wide grin split Jeremy's face.

"And that's great news? It sounds like pretty sucky news to me." I took a swig of my champagne.

"That's where you're wrong. Well, not wrong precisely. It does suck for her about the leg, but it's good news for us. Angie was going to supervise the volunteers at the Theater in the Pines this summer."

My heart warmed at fond memories of volunteering as an usher at the local summer stock theater, which managed to attract some big name acts and shows. Due to our relative proximity to Broadway, a lot of plays used to do a trial run at the Theater in the Pines to work out the kinks before they took their show to the big time.

"Theater in the Pines." I heaved a sigh of contentment. "Some of my happiest memories are of the three of us working there in the summer."

"Me too. Which is why when the opportunity to manage it this summer came up, I jumped on it. Usually when school lets out, I just hang around all summer, because Eric still has to work, so we can't travel anywhere."

Jeremy taught English and drama at our alma mater, Hills Regional High School.

"It's a perfect fit for you," Cara said.

"And now for Amanda. With my volunteer coordinator out of commission, I find myself in need of a qualified person to take her place." He stared fixedly at me.

"Is it part-time?" I asked.

"It is. And mostly in the late afternoon and early evening, which would leave you most of the day to write. What do you say, Amanda? Will you take the job?" He extended his hand to me.

I grasped it in a firm shake, bubbles of happiness as potent as the champagne now tickling my heart. "I will. I'm so excited. Thank you, Jeremy. It's perfect."

Cara screwed up her mouth and squinted at Jeremy. "Almost too perfect. You didn't trip Angie to get her to break her leg, did you?"

He held his hands over his heart. "I'm deeply offended you would think that of me. I might joke about it, but I would probably never trip someone for personal gain."

"Probably never?" I raised my eyebrows and looked Jeremy up and down.

He laughed and waved his hands at me. "She broke it skateboarding. I was nowhere near the scene."

I jumped up and threw my arms around Jeremy's neck, which made Fluffy start barking again. "Thank you so much, Jeremy. I'll do a great job for you. You won't regret hiring me."

Cara raised her glass in another toast. "Now you can really begin this next part of your life. To Amanda."

"To Amanda Seldon's Second Act. Which is always the best part of the play. It's when all the exciting stuff happens." Jeremy clinked his glass to Cara's.

My heart fluttered in my chest, and I sent a fervent wish out to the universe Jeremy was right and this would be when exciting stuff happened in my life. Things had been routine for too long in my world.

I brought mine up to theirs. "To my second act."

Chapter Two

I opened the passenger side window and let the fresh air wash over me as Jeremy turned into the road next to a rustic, carved wooden sign for the Theater in the Pines.

"You look like a dog. Why don't you stick your head all the way out and pant?" Jeremy slanted a glance my way.

"Hey, *you* live in LA for ten years and then tell me how much you appreciate smog-free air."

"Valid point. Even after I'd visit you there I was always glad to get home. I guess I'm just not a city boy at heart."

The log cabin style theater loomed before us as we rounded the last bend. The parking area was mostly empty compared to a show night, but there was a smattering of vehicles parked in the lot. "Is there a rehearsal happening today?"

"Yes. It's why I thought today would be a good day to bring you round to meet everybody. The crew is here, as well as the cast," Jeremy said.

"The crew aren't local people?"

He shook his head as he eased his SUV into a spot

near the entrance. "Not for this show. It's a preview run before they open on Broadway."

"That's kind of a big deal, isn't it?"

Jeremy turned off the car, but didn't exit. He turned in his seat to look at me. "It is. When we were kids it happened more often. But now Theater in the Pines does more summer stock-type theater, which I enjoy more than this show, to tell you the truth."

"How come?"

"The director is notoriously difficult. Word around the summer theater circuit is lots of places claimed they were booked solid to avoid working with him." He grimaced. "We may or may not be a last resort for them."

I panned my hands across the air in front of me. "*Theater in the Pines—we might be your last choice, but we're happy to have you.* Could be our new slogan."

Jeremy snickered. "We're happy to have them, but their tech crew is miserable here. We're still a hemp house, and a lot of them don't like it."

"Hemp house?" I wrinkled my nose. "So the crew is anti-drugs? Doesn't seem like a bad thing."

"Not a drug den. It just means we still use the old-fashioned hemp ropes, rather than the newer motorized systems. Very few theaters are still hemp houses, so a lot of the crew aren't experienced with the equipment."

I nudged his shoulder and waggled my eyebrows. "They're learning the ropes then?"

He rolled his eyes as dramatically as a teenager exasperated by a parent, and opened his car door. "That's really bad. True, but a lousy joke."

We both exited the car and strolled toward the entrance. "How difficult could the director be that an entire crew is having to learn an old rigging system because no other theaters would have him?" I playfully punched

Jeremy's bicep. "Hey! Another slogan idea. *When no other theater will have you ... come to the Theater in the Pines.*"

"I'll let you see for yourself. There's been more drama offstage than on it so far." He held the door open.

Stepping into the lobby was like stepping back in time. It looked exactly like it did in my teen years when I used to volunteer here. Roughhewn beams and a soaring ceiling managed to make the space seem both grand and cozy at the same time. The box office was to the right, the restrooms to the left, and ahead of us was a bank of open doors to the theater itself.

Angry voices broke my reverie with the past and dragged me back to the present.

"You're killing my work. My words. My essence. I should do the same to you!"

JEREMY THREW UP HIS HANDS AND RACED INTO THE theater. "Gentlemen, gentlemen, you're arguing again?"

I followed him to see two men standing in front of the stage. Both turned to look at Jeremy. One of them was so handsome I assumed he was the lead actor. Tall and slender with blond hair, ice-blue eyes, and cheekbones that could slice paper. He shrugged at Jeremy and jerked his head at the other man.

The man Mr. Cheekbones was arguing with raked his hands through his unruly dark hair, which made it stand out in every direction. "Jeremy, maybe you can talk some sense into him. He's turned my work into a farce."

As we reached the two men, the handsome one gave me an appraising once-over. Yuck. *Welcome to the twenty-first century buddy. Women are more than just eye candy.* The dark-haired man turned his gaze to me, and his eyes could only be described as wild. Deep sunk and below bushy eyebrows, they darted between Jeremy and me.

Ignoring both the angry man and my clear not-interested signals, the handsome man smirked at me and held out his hand. "I'm Aaron Hillner, the director of *Ecstasy in the Aspens*—"

"*Agony in the Aspens*." Wild-eyes interrupted. "The title is *Agony in the Aspens*."

Hillner heaved a sigh and lowered his hand. He glared at the other man. "The title of your book is *Agony in the Aspens*, but the title of this play is *Ecstasy in the Aspens*." He turned to me and flashed a smile of blindingly white teeth. "We've made some changes to Mr. Dickens's work, and he is not pleased."

"Mr. Dickens?" I glanced at Wild-eyes.

"Melville Dickens, I wrote the novel upon which this monstrosity of a play is based."

"Your name is Melville Dickens?" I asked.

Hillner snorted. "Ridiculous, isn't it?"

"I wanted to honor my idols, Herman Melville and Charles Dickens, so I legally changed my name. It is most decidedly not ridiculous. What is ridiculous is this farce you've created from the finely woven fabric of my work."

Jeremy had not exaggerated when he said there was more drama offstage than on it. The cast stood on the stage and watched the spectacle unfolding before them in front of the seats.

A man's deep voice boomed behind me. "People, people. You're the cast not the audience. Get back to rehearsal."

Everyone jumped at his command, and even Dickens and Hillner stopped arguing, although rage was still etched on the author's gaunt face. I turned to see the man who could command such immediate attention. An older gentleman with a mane of luxuriant white hair strode down the aisle. He was very distinguished and impeccably dressed in a well-fitted suit that had to have been made to order.

Jeremy stood a little straighter and pasted a smile on his face. I'd known my friend long enough to recognize it wasn't sincere, but no one else could probably tell. "Mr. Adams. I didn't know you'd be joining us today."

The man had reached our awkward little group. "Hello, Jeremy. My visit is a surprise." He adjusted his cuffs as he looked around the theater. "Rumors have reached me in New York about the production being in complete disarray. I see I was not misled. Aaron, why on earth are you arguing with Mr. Dickens in front of the troupe? Where is your dignity? As the director of the play you set the tone."

Two spots of red appeared on Aaron's high cheekbones. "I'm sorry, Pen. I shouldn't have lost my temper. But this hack—" he pointed to Melville, and his voice again rose in anger. "Has been relentless in his criticism of the play. It's interfering with our work every day."

Mr. Adams turned his gaze to Melville Dickens. "Is this true?"

Melville waved his hands in the air. "Of course it's true. You people are murdering my creation. *Agony in the Aspens* was not meant to be a light, musical romp."

"Let me interject here," Mr. Adams held up one hand in a graceful gesture, and Melville snapped his jaw shut with an audible click. "You signed a contract, did you not?"

"I did."

"And our contract stipulated you have absolutely no say in the script of the production. It is loosely based on your work—"

Melville snorted in derision, and Mr. Adams's gaze could've frozen over Orchard Pond in July.

"As I was saying, while *Ecstasy in the Aspens* is an interpretation of your original work, creative control is now completely in our capable hands. If you continue to disrupt production, I am going to be forced to get a restraining order to keep you away, and no one wants that, do they?"

The author scuffed the toe of his ratty sneaker on the floor. "No, sir."

Adams clasped his hands together and beamed. "Splendid. We're all friends again."

I glanced at Hillner and Dickens, who glared like two prize fighters trying to psyche each other out before a bout and was dubious they would ever be friends. Melville stomped up the aisle, took a seat in the middle of the theater, folded his arms across his chest, and scowled at the stage.

"Mr. Penrose Adams, I'd like you to meet Amanda Seldon. She's our new part-time volunteer coordinator at the Theater in the Pines," Jeremy said.

We shook hands, and I winced at the strength of the producer's firm grip. "It's a pleasure to meet you, Mr. Adams."

"Please call me Pen." He bestowed a warm smile upon me, but as he turned to look at Hillner, he frowned. "Aaron. I'd like to speak to you in private, please."

"Certainly, sir. Let me just tell the cast to take five."

Before he could do so a frantic cry sounded from the rigging high above the stage. "Heads! Heads!"

THE CAST SCATTERED AS THEY EACH CALLED OUT, "THANK you."

A large piece of scenery flew across the back of the stage from left to right. I nibbled my bottom lip, as I strained to remember my old volunteer days at the theater. I guess it would be more accurate to say the huge canvas piece traveled from stage right to stage left.

Pen put his hands on his hips and glared up into the lights at the rigging. "I see the crew has not adapted well to working in a hemp house?"

"It's been an adjustment," Aaron acknowledged with a faint grimace.

Pen looked at Jeremy. "May Aaron and I use your office for our conversation?"

"Of course, sir." Jeremy stood a little straighter.

As the two men walked away, and the crew scrambled to wrangle the out-of-control scenery into submission, I whistled low between my teeth. "You weren't kidding about the drama."

A pretty young woman pranced up the aisle. "Hiya, Mr. Patterson."

"Hello, Kaylee. We won't need the ushers until we open. Speaking of ushers, I'd like you to meet Amanda Seldon. You'll be reporting to her from now on." He smiled at me. "Amanda, this is Kaylee Tufton, a former student of mine at the high school, who is one of your ushers this summer."

We smiled and shook hands. Her long, pointy fingernails poked into my palm when we did. She was fresh faced and lovely, in a wholesome way. Her honey-colored hair swung over her shoulders. Wearing denim shorts, a shell pink tank top, and snowy white sneakers on her feet, she didn't strike me as the kind of girl who'd have the trendy manicure.

"Nice to meet you, Kaylee. Happy to have you ushering here this summer. I did too when I was in high school."

Her bright green eyes opened wide, and her pink lips formed a perfect 'O'. "I'm not in high school, ma'am."

"Kaylee is about to embark on her senior year of college," Jeremy said with a fond smile at his former student.

"That's right. I don't know how you could possibly have thought I was a high schooler." Kaylee raised her chin, and I think the lofty tone of voice she used was supposed to be sophisticated, but just sounded petulant.

Jeremy winked at me. "When you're as old as Ms. Selden, everyone seems younger."

"Hey! We're the same age," I said.

"I'm old too." Jeremy shrugged. He turned his gaze back to Kaylee. "So what are you doing here today?"

"I just wanted to watch the rehearsal. It's so fascinating to see Aaron ... umm ... Mr. Hillner work." Her cheeks grew as pink as her shirt.

"Okay, well don't get in the way," Jeremy waved his index finger.

"No, sir. I won't."

"Amanda, let me show you to your office," he said.

When we got several rows away from Kaylee, I whispered, "Looks like someone has a crush on the director."

"I do not. He might be handsome, but he's a total jerk," Jeremy responded.

"I meant Kaylee, you goofball." I swatted at his arm, and he dodged out of the way. "What was the deal when the scenery went rogue? Why did the cast say 'thank you'?"

"When there's a runaway lineset, the flyperson is supposed to yell 'heads' to warn the people onstage. Well, actually he's supposed to indicate more details about which lineset has gone runaway, but there usually isn't time to say more than 'heads.'"

"And what's with the thank-yous?"

"It's the standard response, so the flyperson knows they've been heard."

"Interesting. I guess it could do a lot of damage with lights and scenery flying around willy-nilly," I said.

We'd reached the lobby and Jeremy gestured to a doorway to the right of the box office. "Yes, it could be devasting. The scenery, lighting, the sandbags are all very heavy and could easily injure someone. Or worse." We reached the door, and he unlocked it and handed me the key. "This is going to be your office for the summer."

"Thanks for the key."

"No worries. It's a small office, but it should be plenty of room. And if you keep her in here, you can bring The Beast with you when you're working during the day. Not during performances though."

"That's great! She went to doggie daycare in LA while I was at work, so she's not used to being alone for long."

Jeremy raised his eyebrows. "She went to doggie daycare and she's still not better socialized?"

"She's progressed by leaps and bounds since she was a puppy. What are you talking about?" I looked around the office, and it took all of one second. "You weren't kidding when you said it was small. This could fit in my old office five times over."

"Well you're not the VP of Human Resources anymore, kiddo. You're an aspiring author and the part-time volunteer coordinator at an old theater in the middle of the forest."

I tossed my purse on the desk. "At least there's a computer, so we're somewhat into the twenty-first century here."

"Too bad the rigging system isn't," Jeremy said with a deep sigh. "It would cost a fortune to upgrade it to a more modern system. But after today, I'm worried it could be a danger with an inexperienced crew."

"Before when you said someone could be injured or worse, what did you mean by worse? Could someone die?"

"Yep. It's why Pen is so worried about the crew having trouble learning how to work with the old hemp fly system. If they don't catch on soon, their inexperience could kill someone."

Chapter Three

I squeezed through the crowd on my way to the bar at Hitchcock's Tavern, the local watering hole in Maple Hills. Not many of the faces were familiar to me. I guess a lot had changed in our little town in the past ten years. A burst of laughter brought my attention to a table of people I did recognize. The cast and crew of *Ecstasy in the Aspens*.

A shrill whistle rent the air, and I jerked my head in its direction. "Amanda! Over here."

Aunt Lori waved her hands in the air like she was guiding in a jet. Like I could've missed her after the whistle and holler. Certainly no man in the bar did. Heads turned to check out my gorgeous aunt. My dad's sister was a good bit younger than him, and was in her mid-fifties now, but we could easily pass for contemporaries.

I returned her wave and shoved my way through the crowd to reach her table, where she immediately enveloped my in a bear hug. "I'm so glad you're home, Mandy-bel."

"Lower your voice. You are literally the only person on the planet who is allowed to call me that name. I don't want anyone else to hear it."

She pulled back, and her laugh tinkled like wind chimes, and her bright green eyes sparkled. "Don't worry, no one can hear a thing in this crush."

A waitress appeared at the table as if by magic. "What can I get you ladies?"

"A dirty martini, emphasis on the dirty," Aunt Lori said with a waggle of her expertly shaped and shaded eyebrows.

"Pear vodka and tonic for me, please."

"You got it." The waitress tucked her pencil behind her ear and elbowed her way to the bar.

We sat down. "How on earth did you get this table? Have you been here since you left work?"

"I've gone out with the manager once or twice. He cleared it for me." She tossed her brown hair streaked with blonde over her shoulder and shrugged.

"You're a good woman to know, Aunt Lori."

"That I am."

The waitress returned with our drinks, and Aunt Lori lifted her glass in a toast. "To my wandering niece returning home."

I clinked my glass with hers, and we sipped our cocktails. "I wasn't exactly wandering. I lived in New York for a couple of years after college and then was transferred to Los Angeles, where I stayed for ten years."

"But aside from your holiday visits, you haven't been back to Maple Hills very often."

My cheeks grew warm. "I know, and I'm sorry. When Dad needed surgery—"

Aunt Lori held up her hands. "No guilt trip here, Mandy-bel. You had a life out there. A bigtime career, a condo, friends... I get it. It's just nice to have you home."

"It's nice to be home. I had a lot of fun with Cara and Jeremy last night."

"The Three Musketeers together again. I like it."

I craned my neck to look around the room. "Is it always so crowded here?"

"Karaoke night. It's always a crush. And trivia night is too. Speaking of, with your mom on the road this summer, my team is down a person. Care to join us?"

Since my aunt was the town librarian, and a font of knowledge, her team was a good one to join. Spots on it were highly prized. "Are you sure you don't have a waiting list?"

"Nepotism wins out yet again. My favorite niece jumps to the head of the line."

"I'm your only niece."

She winked at me. "You'd be my favorite even if I had one hundred nieces. So, how about it? You in?"

"I'm in, as long as trivia night doesn't fall on a night I need to be at the theater."

"That's right. Jeremy told me you were working there part-time this summer. Are you sure it won't interfere with your writing?"

"I don't think so. I even have a little office there I can write in, if I feel like it. And I can bring Fluffy with me."

Aunt Lori's eyes bugged. "The Beast? You would unleash her on an unwitting public in the theater?"

I smacked her hand. "Fluffy is a sweetheart when she gets to know you."

"And an adorable little terror until she does." My aunt turned in her seat, stared, and jerked her chin toward the raucous table from the Theater in the Pines. "Those folks are all from the show, aren't they? Who's the gorgeous blond guy? Let me guess ... he's the leading man."

"Nope. He's the director, Aaron Hillner."

"And I recognize the girl next to him hanging on his

every word. She's a local. Kaylee Tufton. What's she doing with that crowd?"

"She's one of my volunteers. She was at the theater today, and I got the distinct impression she has a serious crush on Hillner. Who seems like kind of a jerk to me."

"But a beautiful jerk. He could be a model. Kaylee has been dating the same boy since they were in middle school, and he's a good kid. But he can't compete with Mr. Hotstuff Director. I hope her crush doesn't hurt their relationship."

"Me too. She seems like a nice kid, and like I said, Hillner doesn't seem like the nicest guy."

"Nothing we can do about it either way, I'd just hate to see a nice young woman like her go down the wrong path. And while it might be a lovely path at first, it won't lead anywhere good." Lori sipped her drink. "So, who are the others?"

"A lot of crew people, whose names I haven't learned yet. The distinguished gentleman is Penrose Adams, he's the producer. And the beautiful redhead on Aaron Hillner's other side is Maisy Lapointe. She's the leading lady."

"And who is the hot mess who looks like he just swallowed a lemon?"

"He's the improbably named Melville Dickens."

Recognition gleamed in Lori's eyes. "I've heard of him. He wrote the novel this play is based on, right? It was very popular for a while there. The library book club read it, so I gave it a whack, but it wasn't my cup of bourbon."

"Don't you mean tea?"

"Potato, potahto." She raised one shoulder and smirked.

Did I mention Aunt Lori defied every librarian stereotype there was? Come to think of it, I never knew a librarian who fit the mold. They were always smart, funny, and most definitely not shushers.

An attractive middle-aged man took the small stage at the front of the room and flashed a roguish grin at Aunt Lori.

"The manager who cleared this table for us?" I asked.

She nodded. "Yep."

He stepped up to the microphone and tapped it once, prompting a squeal of feedback. "Ladies and Gentlemen, welcome to karaoke night at the Hitchcock Tavern. Who wants to be first up tonight?"

Maisy Lapointe jumped to her feet. "Me!"

The actress slithered through the crowd with a serpentine grace to the small stage and whispered something to the manager, who entered her song choice into the karaoke machine. She surveyed the room in the way actors do, which makes every audience member believe they are the center of the performer's focus. Her gaze settled on Aaron Hillner, and she blew him a flirtatious kiss when the chords of a romantic power ballad filled the bar.

She purred into the microphone. "This one is for Aaron."

Kaylee's face flushed red as a ripe apple as she glared at Maisy.

"My, my, my. Our little Kaylee is shooting daggers at the leading lady." Aunt Lori looked between the two women like she was at a tennis match.

I nodded. "I think I know where the expression 'if looks could kill' comes from now. It looks like they didn't leave all the drama at the theater."

Engrossed in Maisy's performance I jumped at a man's voice behind me.

"Amanda, how nice to see you this evening. And who is your lovely companion?"

Penrose Adams stood over my right shoulder and beamed at Aunt Lori.

"Hello, Mr. Adams."

"Please call me Pen."

"Then, hello, Pen. This is my aunt, Lori Seldon. Aunt Lori, this is the producer of the play at the Theater in the Pines, Penrose Adams." I went through the whole charade of an introduction, because there was no need for Pen to know we were gossiping about his table over cocktails and Aunt Lori already knew full well who he was.

He skirted the table and took the hand Aunt Lori extended and kissed it in a courtly gesture. "A pleasure to meet you, Lori. May I call you Lori?"

"Certainly, Pen." Aunt Lori bestowed a queenly smile on Pen.

Since her divorce, she'd had no shortage of suitors panting after her, so I guess she'd learned to accept their praise as her due.

When Pen turned his back on us to drag a chair to the table, she winked at me. Merriment twinkled in her eyes. No one enjoyed life like my Aunt Lori did. Even the most routine events were fun when she was involved.

"Maisy has an amazing singing voice," I said.

"Very powerful and passionate," Aunt Lori added.

Pen looked away from the stage and turned his attention back to us. Who am I kidding? He turned his attention back to Aunt Lori.

"Her passion seems to be putting her on the wrong side of our little theater intern." Pen glanced at Kaylee before gazing back into Lori's eyes.

"But the man she dedicated the song to is eating it up with a spoon," Aunt Lori said.

"Aaron loves the attention of the fairer sex, which is

most unfortunate for his long-suffering wife." Pen frowned at Hillner.

I watched Maisy as she reached a crescendo, and her porcelain complexion flushed. Her attention shifted from Aaron to a woman approaching his table.

Elegant and exotically beautiful, with jet black hair arranged in a low, loose bun on the back of her swanlike neck. Her whole look screamed Manhattan socialite. And Maisy Lapointe couldn't look more annoyed to see her heading toward Aaron like a guided missile than if she were ...well, really a guided missile.

"Oh my, you ladies will have to excuse me." Pen rose from the table, his attention riveted on the newcomer.

"Is that Mrs. Adams?" I asked.

He shook his head. "No, my dear. She is Magdalena Hillner. Aaron's wife."

MAISY FINISHED HER NUMBER AND RAN TO AARON'S SIDE. Unaware his wife had entered the room, he stood up and threw his arms around Maisy, who planted a passionate kiss on his lips.

"Poor little Kaylee." Aunt Lori tsked her tongue. "She looks like she's about to burst into tears. These crushes are so powerful at her age. I wouldn't be twenty-one again for anything."

Pen forced his way through the crowd in an attempt to reach Magdalena before she got to her husband and his mini harem of female admirers.

Magdalena narrowed her eyes at her husband and elbowed a young man out of her way to get to the table. It was a move worthy of a roller derby star, and was unexpected for such a glamorous woman.

"Oh my gosh, this is like watching a silent movie," I said.

Lori leaned forward and bobbed her head. "I know. I wish we were closer so we could hear them."

The maneuver was enough to prevent Pen from reaching her in time, and Magdalena grabbed her husband's shoulder and jerked him around. His expression would have been comical if not for the fact real emotions were at play. His eyes bugged out of his head, and his jaw dropped to the floor. To his benefit, he recovered quickly and forced a smile to his face as he greeted his wife with a kiss. Or tried to. Magdalena turned her head at the last second, and he merely brushed her cheek with his lips. Undeterred, he put his arm around her shoulders and introduced her to the table.

As Magdalena coolly greeted Maisy, who looked as gobsmacked as Aaron and less successful at hiding it, Kaylee jumped up from the table and knocked over her chair in the process. The poor young woman burst into tears and ran for the exit.

Aunt Lori stood up and grinned down at me. "I think it's about time you took me over to introduce me to your new coworkers."

"Now? In the middle of this scene?"

"What better time?"

Aunt Lori grabbed my hands and tugged me to my feet, and I followed in her wake as she effortlessly cleared the way to the theater company's table.

All heads turned to us. I waved in a half-hearted manner. "Hi. Remember me? Amanda Seldon from the Theater in the Pines? My aunt and I were here tonight also, and I wanted her to meet you all."

Pen beamed at me as if I were a toddler who'd just spoken her first words. "How thoughtful of you. Join us, ladies. Please." He opened his eyes wide as if willing us to sit. It seemed like Pen was all too happy to draw attention away from the scene which had been unfolding at the table.

"If you insist," Lori said as she righted the chair Kaylee had so unceremoniously knocked over and sat down.

One of the crew tugged another chair over for me, and I squeezed in between Lori and Aaron.

"You're just in time to meet my wife. Amanda, this is Magdalena Hillner. Darling, Amanda is the volunteer coordinator at the theater."

"And this is my aunt, Lori Seldon. She's the librarian here in town," I said.

As if he weren't already in enough trouble, Aaron's gaze took a leisurely trip up and down Aunt Lori's body, and he waggled his eyebrows. "If I'd ever seen a librarian as gorgeous as you, I would have spent a lot more time checking out ... books." He paused just long enough to make it clear reading material wasn't all he would be checking out at the library.

Magdalena snorted and even made the coarse noise elegant. She then turned to me and extended her hand. "Very nice to meet you, Amanda."

And it probably was nice for her, as I appeared to be the one woman at the table her husband wasn't coming on to.

Speaking of, Maisy looked at her smartwatch and jumped up from the table. "Look at the time, I need to get back to the Inn."

"Surely not so soon, dear." Magdalena arched one eyebrow, and her crimson lips curved into a sly smile. "I caught the tail end of your number when I arrived. Very moving. I was hoping for an encore."

Maisy's cheeks flushed, and Aaron scowled at his wife. I squirmed in my seat. Since the actress's number had been a passionate love song dedicated to Magdalena's husband, the moment was off-the-charts awkward.

"What are you doing here, Magdalena?" Aaron asked.

"I wanted to surprise you, dearest heart." She tapped her chin with a long, pointy nail painted in a neutral taupe color. "And look at what a good job I did."

Maisy grabbed her purse off the back of her chair and stammered her excuses before fleeing as if a pack of angry wolves were at her heels.

"Oh dear, it appears I've scared two of your girlfriends away. Should I go for three?" She glanced at Aunt Lori, who surprised us all by barking out a laugh.

"I'm just here enjoying my niece's company. No need to scare me. And even if there were, I don't scare easily."

I cleared my throat. "On that note, we better get back to our table before someone poaches it. Aunt Lori?"

My aunt rose and smiled at Pen. "It was so nice to meet you, Pen. If you have time, please stop by the library."

Melville Dickens raised his head at her words. "Do you have my book in your collection? *Agony in the Aspens*."

"We do. It was very popular with our patrons. It was even a book club read here in town."

The author ran his hand through his already messy hair and smiled. I realized it was the first time I'd seen him do so.

"Would you like me to autograph a copy for you?"

"That would be marvelous. Thank you. Please come to the library anytime and ask for me. You can't miss it. It's the big, brick building right on the town square."

We said our goodbyes and managed to get back to our table before we both burst out laughing. We collapsed into

our seats, and Aunt Lori grasped my arm as we both struggled to catch our breath.

"This has already been the most interesting evening
I've had in a long time, and you've only been here for half
an hour." She paused to catch her breath, and beamed at
me. "I'm going to love having you back in town, Mandy-
bel."

Chapter Four

"C'mon, Fluffy. Isn't it bad enough you woke me up before the sun this morning, now you're going to dawdle here at the theater. Spoiler alert, it's called the Theater in the Pines because it is surrounded by trees. You don't have to sniff every one of them."

Fluffy didn't even spare me a glance as she continued her inspection of a pine tree. I glanced around and noticed the parking lot was empty except for one flashy, red sports car with New York license plates. It had Aaron Hillner written all over it, which didn't thrill me. I had come in early today to write, because Jeremy had told me rehearsals didn't start until one o'clock.

I'd been looking forward to the peace and quiet of my office as a place to get some online research done for the historical fiction book I was writing. I hadn't found a good place to work yet at my parents' house. My teenaged bedroom was out; it brought back memories of doing homework in high school. The kitchen table wasn't the most comfortable spot to sit at all day, and the deck was less than optimal. The weather was too variable, and I got distracted out there. One day I sat and watched hummingbirds at my mom's feeder for way too long. So, here I was. But of all the people to be at the theater, Aaron was the worst possible one.

The man seemed to have two settings, flirtatious or arrogant jerk, and I wasn't crazy about either one of them. Hopefully, if Aaron was here early, it was because he had work to do too. If I was lucky, he would leave me alone.

The leash slackened in my hand, and Fluffy's collar jingled as she trotted back to me. The sunlight showed the red streaks in her black fur. She was definitely not show dog quality, and the hint of brownish-red in her black fur was only one reason. Her black and white fur was also too curly, which is why I kept it trimmed in a shorter puppy cut. And as the runt of the litter, even fully grown, she was on the small side. But Fluffy and I were a team, and I couldn't love her more.

"Good girl. Let's go inside, and I'll get you settled in my office. Then I'll run back out for your stuff." I'd bought a water dish and dog bed to keep in my office for Fluffy.

I dug in my pocket for the key to the theater Jeremy had given me, but as we approached the row of doors which led to the lobby, I noticed one of them was wide open. I remembered from my days as a teenaged volunteer here, on show nights we would open all the doors for people to enter. One of my jobs was closing them once the show began, opening them again at intermission, closing them once everyone was reseated and repeating the process at the end of the show. In retrospect, a lot of my time as a volunteer was spent opening and closing these rough-hewn, wooden doors.

Why did Aaron, if it was his car out front, leave a door open? The theater was air-conditioned, so it couldn't be for fresh air. And how much fresh air would reach him in the theater with just one door open in the lobby? Maybe the big shot director usually had minions to do tasks like shutting doors for him and was lost without their assistance here 'in the country', as city people always referred to Maple Hills.

We entered the lobby, and I turned immediately to my right to go to my office. If at all possible, I wanted to avoid speaking with Aaron Hillner. But Fluffy had other ideas and trotted toward the theater. She was twelve pounds of determined dog, and while I tried to steer her in the direction I wanted to go, she wasn't having it.

"Fluffy, where are you going?"

I stopped walking, but she kept going until she'd reached the limit of her leash and continued to tug until she choked a little.

"What are you doing, girl? You'll hurt yourself." I relented and moved closer to her.

Fluffy took advantage of the slack in her leash to run forward a few more steps until she was right at the doorway from the lobby into the theater. She turned back toward me, her pink tongue poking out as she panted.

"Impatient much? Jeez, I'm coming." I decided to go where she wanted to because she was the most single-minded little creature and wouldn't settle down until I did. Spoiled? Perhaps.

The little dog tugged me up the aisle toward the stage. Her huffs of breath and claws clicking on the wooden floor were the only sounds in the empty theater.

Empty theater? Where was Aaron Hillner, or whoever owned the sports car in the lot? If no one was here, why was the front door open when I'd arrived?

I frowned and glanced up from Fluffy, where my attention had been focused, to look around for any signs of life.

The determined shih tzu kept pulling me toward the stage, and I noticed ropes dangling from the rafters.

What happened there? Had something fallen?

And that's when I noticed it. Him. The body.

A man was sprawled on the stage floor, buried underneath a huge piece of lighting equipment.

I gasped, and the sound was freakishly loud in the empty theater. Fluffy began to bark, a surprisingly deep, raspy sound for such a tiny dog. People were always surprised when they heard her.

The stage had stairs on either end which led to the seating area of the theater. I rushed toward one of them, Fluffy's ears blown back as she pumped her short legs to keep up with me. Was Aaron Hillner underneath the large light, or was it someone else?

One of the reasons I was good at my previous career was I kept my head in a crisis. However, seeing the too-still body, with his head under the heavy piece of lighting equipment tested the limits of my calm. My heart raced, and sweat beads formed at my hairline.

To calm myself, I took deep breaths and tried to reason out the situation. Was there any chance the person was alive? Perhaps the light had just knocked him out, or trapped him. And who was it?

"Are you all right?" I called.

Silence greeted my question.

As I got closer I noticed the expensive Italian loafers, worn with no socks. I'd noticed his shoes yesterday when I met him. I swallowed hard. It was Aaron Hillner.

"Mr. Hillner? Aaron, are you okay? What happened?"

Still no answers, but by now I was next to him. My heart sank as I surveyed the scene. The black metal lighting fixture appeared to be the largest of the lights used to illuminate the stage, and it sat squarely on his head.

"Please say something. Are you conscious?" I squatted next to him and grasped his wrist to check for a pulse.

The bagel I'd treated myself to for breakfast this morning roiled in my stomach. There was no pulse and his flesh was cold.

Aaron Hillner was most definitely not conscious. As a matter of fact, he was dead.

Fluffy and I waited in the lobby for emergency services to arrive. It was too late for an ambulance to do any good, but when I called nine-one-one, they told me they'd be sending police and an ambulance.

Guilt stabbed at my heart about leaving Aaron alone like that, but I couldn't bear to stay in the theater and look at his body displayed on the stage like some sort of grotesque performance art.

I hit Jeremy's name on my speed dial.

"Hey, Amanda. What's up?"

"I'm at the theater, and there's a problem here."

"What kind of problem? Is the power out? Honestly if there's just a stiff breeze, the lights will flicker there."

"It's not the lights. Well, it *is* a light, but not the electricity." My voice trailed off, and I snuffled.

"You're scaring me. What's happening."

"Someone is on the stage; I'm pretty sure it's Aaron Hillner. And he was crushed by a piece of lighting equipment." I paused to gulp. "He's dead, Jeremy."

"I'm on my way. Is anyone else there?"

"Just Fluffy and me. Police and an ambulance are on the way." The wail of sirens punctuated my words as they grew louder. "I think they're here. I better hang up. Get here soon though, please. I could use another Musketeer right about now."

Two EMTs rushed through the door, followed by a policeman who looked vaguely familiar to me. Maybe we went to high school together, although he looked a few years older than me.

"Where is he?" One of the EMTs asked.

I pointed toward the theater. "In there. On the stage."

They all bustled past me, and Fluffy and I trailed after them. I didn't want to be a big baby and stay in the lobby. It seemed wrong.

They were all on the stage surrounding the body as I forced myself to walk up the aisle. The policeman looked up and locked eyes with me.

"You're the one who found him?"

I nodded. "Yes. I'm Amanda Seldon, the volunteer coordinator for the theater. I was coming in early, because there wasn't a rehearsal until later today. I wanted to get some work done."

The man narrowed his eyes at me as he rose from beside the body. "I know who you are, Ms. Seldon."

"You do? You look familiar to me too. Did we go to high school together?"

He sauntered across the stage and down the stairs. "You were in my little brother's class. Dylan Carlow."

My heart raced. Huh. After all these years, the mention of Dylan's name could still get the old ticker thumping. I'd had such a massive crush on him back in the day, but the handsome athlete hadn't even known I was alive.

"Right, Dylan. I remember him." I strove for casual, but my voice betrayed me with a squeak. "Your family owns Maple Hills Orchard, right?"

"Yep. Dylan is running the family business now. I didn't know you were back in town." The policeman reached my side. "I'm Danny Carlow, by the way. I'm the police chief now."

Fluffy positioned herself in front of me and growled low in her throat, and Danny flinched. "She's a fierce little thing."

I scooped her up and held her in my arms. "Sorry. She's very protective of me."

Danny furrowed his brow as he looked at Fluffy, who burrowed her head underneath my chin. It was her way of hugging me. "Seems calm enough now. Tell me what happened here from the beginning."

"I don't know. He was dead when I got here." I recounted the story of how Fluffy and I arrived at the theater and found Aaron's body.

He ran his hand over his mouth and peered up at the dangling rope.

One of the EMTs stood up and said, "Looks like he was alone on the stage, and this rope gave way, causing the light to fall on him."

I glanced at Aaron and wrinkled my nose. "Why isn't there blood? I mean, if a big light like that one fell on your head, wouldn't there be a lot of blood?" I'm glad there wasn't, as I probably would've fainted at the sight, and the next person to arrive at the theater would've found both of us unconscious on the stage.

"Not necessarily." the EMT said.

"Really?" I asked.

The other EMT nodded as he rose. "Yep. It looks like the round glass over the light is what hit him, not the sharp metal. So the force could've shoved his skull into his brain and killed him without breaking the skin."

Allrighty, there was a mental image designed to keep me awake tonight.

"We'll have to wait for the autopsy, but there is almost

certainly internal bleeding from the traumatic brain injury," his partner added.

Footsteps pounded in the lobby, and we all looked in that direction. Jeremy charged in, wearing a ratty Hills Regional High School tee shirt, in the school colors of burgundy with HRHS printed in white across the front, and a pair of baggy workout shorts. I must've interrupted his morning workout when I called.

"I'm here, Amanda. Are you okay?" He panted.

"The Three Musketeers are still as tight as ever, I see." Danny scowled at Jeremy and me.

"Hi, Chief Carlow. I'm managing the theater this summer, so Amanda called me after she called nine-one-one."

Another siren screeched from the parking lot, followed by two more officers entering the scene.

"Crime scene investigation? Isn't this just a tragic accident? I mean the rope frayed and the light fell. End of story," the taller EMT said.

Danny glanced at Jeremy and me before he answered. "Not quite." He jerked his head toward the rope. "Take a closer look. It looks like a fairly new rope. Why would it fray?"

Jeremy squinted at the rope. "You're right, Danny. The owner replaced all the rope before this summer season, so there would be no reason for it to fray."

The chief screwed up his mouth and stared at the rope, as if it could speak and tell him what happened. "Could it have been a faulty rope? This is your first production of the season, right? If there was a defect in the rope, this might've been the first opportunity to learn about it."

"It is our first show, so it's possible." Jeremy paled and swiped his hand over his mouth.

I reached out and squeezed his arm. "We don't know that's what happened."

"But if it is, it's the theater's fault Aaron died. And I'm the theater manager." His voice broke at the end.

Chief Carlow took a deep breath and looked Jeremy straight in the eyes. "We don't know what happened yet, buddy. Don't let your mind go there. Let us conduct our investigation and determine what caused the light to fall." He lowered his voice and continued, "And just between us, I'm not convinced the rope just frayed. And if it was cut then this was murder."

"AARON, WHERE ARE YOU?" A WOMAN'S VOICE CALLED from the lobby area.

Fluffy emitted a sharp bark, and I gently shushed her.

"Who's she?" Chief Carlow asked.

I craned my neck to look and saw the lithe silhouette of Magdalena Hillner in the doorway. "It's the dead man's wife."

"Where is my husband, and why are there so many emergency vehicles out front?" She approached us.

The chief held up both hands. "Please don't come any farther ma'am."

Her gaze darted between all of us, and she froze when it reached the EMTs on stage next to her husband's body under the light. She gasped and held her hands over her mouth.

"Mrs. Hillner, please come with me to my office." Jeremy approached her and tried to shepherd her out of the theater, but she refused to budge.

"Is that my husband up there?" Magdalena whispered.

"Let's step out to the lobby." Chief Carlow's voice softened a bit, and he approached the widow in a slow, cautious manner. As if she were a wounded animal he'd come across in the forest.

She allowed herself to be led out of the theater by the chief.

Jeremy and I exchanged a glance, which was all it took for us to understand each other after a lifetime of friendship, and we both scurried after them to the lobby. Neither of us wanted to miss what happened next. It seemed a little ghoulish, even to me, but I'd never been on the scene of a crime before, and it was fascinating, if also horrific. But if I focused on the fascinating aspects of it, then I wouldn't dissolve into tears at the horrific part.

When we reached the lobby, Jeremy steered me off toward his office. "We can listen here, without being too obvious," he whispered.

"Are we awful people?" I asked in low tones.

He shook his head and glanced toward the chief and Mrs. Hillner, who had begun to cry quietly. Chief Carlow looked at us with his eyes wide and jerked his head toward the widow.

"I think he wants us to help," I whispered.

Jeremy was already on the way. "Why don't we step outside to get some air, Mrs. Hillner? There are benches out front, so you can sit down."

Fluffy recognized one of her favorite words in his sentence—outside—and squirmed in my arms. I put her down, but kept a tight grip on her leash and followed the others outside. I blinked in the bright sun as I exited the dimly lit theater.

I heard the thrum of an engine, and the crunch of the gravel parking lot as a car pulled into the spot next to the red sports car. With a frown, I surveyed the rest of the lot. Aside from Jeremy's SUV and my car, the emergency vehicles, and the black, luxury SUV that had just arrived, there was no other car. How had Magdalena gotten here?

The newcomer threw open the door of their SUV, and Fluffy barked furiously. The chief frowned at me, and I mouthed the word 'sorry'. I picked up Fluffy and held her in the crook of my left arm, while stroking her velvety head with my right hand to soothe her. Fortunately, it worked, and she settled in with a delicate, contented snort.

Pen Adams trotted toward Magdalena, where she sat on a wooden bench in front of the theater. "What in the Sam Hill is going on here? Magdalena, are you all right?"

"I may never be all right again, Pen." She delicately dabbed at her eyes with a tissue. "Aaron is dead."

"What?" Pen roared. "He was fine this morning at breakfast, what happened to him?"

The chief straightened up and looked Pen up and down. "You had breakfast with Mr. Hillner this morning? May I ask who you are?"

"I'm the producer of this show, Penrose Adams, and I demand to know what is going on this instant." He looked down his nose at the chief.

To his credit, Carlow didn't flinch under the imperious stare. "I'm Chief Daniel Carlow of the Maple Hills Police Department, and I'll be asking the questions, Mr. Adams."

Jeremy held his hand over his mouth to hide his smile and whispered so only I could hear, "Go, Danny."

Before the chief could begin his questioning, Magdalena said with a sob in her voice, "It's terrible, Pen. Aaron was crushed by a light onstage."

Pen paled, and he plopped in the seat next to Magdalena, all the wind taken out of his sails at her statement. "I knew the crew was struggling working in a hemp house, but I didn't realize things were so bad."

Chief Carlow narrowed his eyes at Pen. "What's a hemp house? Are we talking about drugs?"

"Of course not," Pen puffed himself back up and got back in his poised groove. "It's an antiquated method of lighting and set rigging, and the one employed here at the Theater in the Pines. Our crew is experienced with more modern methods and are having a bit of a steep learning curve. I assume it's why there was such a tragic accident." He patted Magdalena's hand. She buried her face in his shoulder, and her body shook with sobs.

I noticed she was dressed in capri-length leggings, walking shoes, and an athletic bra/top type thing. She looked like she was dressed for a workout. I wondered how and why she'd come to the theater this morning.

"We'll be investigating the cause of Mr. Hillner's death," Chief Carlow said.

Pen straightened up and stared at the police chief. "What do you mean? It's an accident, surely."

"Perhaps." The chief inclined his head. "Perhaps not."

Magdalena sat up, and Pen pulled a handkerchief out of the pocket of his navy sports coat with a courtly gesture and handed it to her. She dabbed at her eyes, which didn't look as wet as they should be, given the sobbing she'd just been doing. "What do you mean? Do you think someone deliberately killed my Aaron?"

The 'my Aaron' might've been laying it on a little thick, as just last night I'd seen him juggling two other woman before his wife arrived, and he still managed to fit in coming on to my Aunt Lori. Perhaps her grief was genuine, or perhaps Magdalena wouldn't miss her cheating husband as much as she wanted us all to believe.

Chapter Five

"I can't believe Aaron Hillner is dead. And Danny Carlow thinks he was murdered?" Aunt Lori's green eyes opened wide, and she leaned back against the circulation desk.

"He certainly thinks it's a possibility," I said.

Once Chief Carlow had released us, Jeremy had gone home to shower and change, and we'd agreed to meet at the Sit and Sip, our local coffee house and key center of gossip in my little hometown. Since I had time before our meeting, I dropped Fluffy at home and raced to the library to fill Aunt Lori in on the morning's events before she heard it from someone else. Because honestly, the Maple Hills Public Library gave the Sit and Sip a run for its money in the town gossip department.

"And you found the body? My poor Mandy-bel."

Aunt Lori pulled me in for a tight hug, and clasped in her loving arms, surrounded by the familiar scent of her expensive perfume, I shuddered as the full impact of what had happened this morning hit me and tears stung at my eyes. "I've never seen a dead person before."

She loosened her grip on me, and I stepped back and grabbed a tissue from a box on the desk and blew my nose at what was surely not a library-approved volume.

"Excuse me, Ms. Seldon?" A man spoke from behind me.

I turned to see none other than Melville Dickens, his hair still a wild mop. He was dressed in baggy plaid shorts, a tee shirt which had clearly seen better days, and a pair of deck shoes.

"Yes," Aunt Lori and I replied in unison. We looked at each other and chuckled.

"I guess I have to get used to having another Ms. Seldon in town for the foreseeable future," Aunt Lori said.

"I meant the librarian," Melville said.

"What can I do for you, Mr. Dickens?" my aunt asked in what I always thought of as her professional librarian voice. It was not soft, but not too loud either, unlike her boisterous everyday manner of speaking, and she managed to convey both friendliness and formality at the same time.

"Last night we'd discussed me autographing your copies of my book. I was at loose ends this morning, so I decided to stop by the library to see if you would like me to sign them."

She clasped her hands. "How wonderful. Let me go gather the copies which are currently here in the library. I'll be right back."

The author bounced on the balls of his feet and looked around the library as if he didn't have a care in the world. If I was a betting woman, I'd wager he hadn't heard about Aaron Hillner's death yet.

"This is a lovely library," he said.

I looked around at the room through his eyes and realized it truly was a beautiful space. Windows lined the exterior walls and faced out over main street and the town square, and the main seating area was set up like a cozy home, complete with a gorgeous fireplace and antique mantel. Comfy looking sofas and chairs dotted the area, along with magazine racks and book displays. The main stacks were behind this area and on the second floor. I'd grown up viewing this library as a home away from home, and I took it for granted. It didn't have any of the 1970's industrial vibe so many libraries did.

"It really is."

An awkward pause ensued. At least it was awkward for me, because I knew about Hillner's death while Dickens obviously did not.

I cleared my throat and asked, "Are you staying at the same hotel as the Hillners and Pen Adams?"

His hair flew out around his head as he shook it vehemently. "No way. They're staying at the fancy inn here in town."

"The Maple Hills Arms?" I asked. The elegant boutique hotel had sprung up in town since I'd moved away from the area. When I lived here, it had been a dumpy hotel, filled with dusty antiques, which were less like what the word implied and more like old, tacky tchotchkes. A company which owned small, elegant inns across the globe had bought it and kept the name, but changed everything else about it.

"That's the place. I'm staying at the Dew Drop Inn outside of town near the lake."

The Dew Drop Inn had seen better days and was mainly used by people coming to fish on the lake, but it was a safe, clean place to stay. My first paying job had been working there as a chambermaid one summer, so I was intimately acquainted with the Dew Drop. More than I'd like to be. Cleaning rooms there, I'd seen some things.

I shuddered and brought my mind back to the present.

"Did you come straight to the library from the Dew Drop this morning?"

He stopped bobbing on his feet and scrunched up his face as he peered at me intently. "That's a funny question. But if you must know, yes, I came directly here."

I swallowed hard. "Then you haven't heard the news?"

"What news?"

"Aaron Hillner is dead." In retrospect I could've broken it to him more gently, but I'd opted for the rip-the-bandage-off method.

"That's not a very funny joke."

"I'm sorry, but it's not a joke, Mr. Dickens. I found his body in the theater this morning."

He took a deep breath, exhaled with a whoosh , and chuckled, which chilled me to my core. Of all his possible reactions to my news, I'd never dreamed he would find it amusing.

"Someone finally killed the despicable reprobate, huh?"

"Why would you assume it was murder and not a heart attack or something?" I edged away from the novelist and closer to the door. His reaction had me wondering if he was capable of murder, and my own heart raced to the point I feared *I* might drop dead of a heart attack right here in the library.

"Because he was young and healthy. And a completely horrible human being."

"Because of what he did to *Agony in the Aspens*?"

"He turned my work into a travesty, an abomination. The man had no sense of great literature. So, yes, I did despise him for what he was doing to my masterpiece."

Enough to kill him?

My thoughts must have shown on my face, because light dawned in his eyes, and he held out his hands. "But I didn't kill him, if that's what you're thinking. You saw him last night. He treated women like nothing more than play-things. Believe you me, there are plenty of people who wanted to kill Aaron Hillner more than I did."

"Here we go, Mr. Dickens," Aunt Lori called out in a singsong voice as she approached with several hardcover books in her hands. "The play has stirred up new interest in your book here in Maple Hills, but we do still have a few copies that aren't checked out for you to sign."

The author perked up at her words and followed her to a table to autograph his work. A chill ran through me as I watched him, and I feared Aunt Lori was having a murderer sign her books.

I GOT TO THE SIT AND SIP BEFORE JEREMY AND ORDERED an iced chai latte for myself and a regular coffee for him. Fortune smiled on me as I walked away from the counter, bobbling both of our drinks, when I spotted two women vacating a table in the corner by the front window. I scooted over and claimed the table for myself.

No sooner had I gotten situated and taken the first sip of my drink than a knock on the window startled me, and I jumped, almost dropping my chai latte. I looked up to see Jeremy's laughing face on the other side of the glass and scowled at him.

He strolled into the restaurant and sat down, still chuckling to himself. "Scaring you like that never gets old. You get so lost in your own thoughts. It's too easy to make you jump." His hair still damp from the shower, Jeremy had changed into a pair of khaki slacks and a navy polo shirt. He picked up his cup and blew on the hot coffee. "Thanks for getting me my coffee."

"You're welcome. If you really wanted to thank me, a kinder way would have been to not startle me and nearly make me spill my drink."

"But so much less funny." He squinted at my drink. "What are you having anyway?"

"An iced chai latte."

He rolled his eyes. "You can take the woman out of Los Angeles..."

"What? It's very refreshing on a hot summer day. More so than hot coffee."

"Where is The Beast?"

"I dropped her at home. She'd had enough excitement for one morning. Then, since I had time to kill—"

"Poor choice of word," Jeremy interrupted.

"Good point. Since I had time to *spare*, I ran by the library to tell Aunt Lori about Aaron. Melville Dickens showed up, and I told him too."

"He hadn't heard yet?" Jeremy held up his index finger. "Hold on, I can answer my own question. He was possibly more unpopular among the cast and crew than Aaron, so I don't imagine anyone would think to tell him."

"It's quite a distinction for him, to be more disliked than Aaron, a man who's just been murdered."

A harsh gasp sounded behind me, followed by a crash. I turned around to see Kaylee Tufton, the theater volunteer with the massive crush on the dead man. Her face was the same shade of white as the coffee mug she'd dropped on the floor and shattered. The clatter of utensils and chatter of the patrons came to an abrupt end, and a sudden silence filled the coffee shop.

"Aaron's been m-m-urdered?" Kaylee's voice was barely a whisper, and she trembled like a leaf.

Jeremy grimaced at me. "Nice move, Amanda." He

jumped up and helped Kaylee into a spare seat at our little café table. "Here, sit down. I'll get you some water."

White shown all around her blue eyes, and she glanced at the broken cup and coffee spilled on the floor. "I dropped my cappuccino. I need to clean it up."

Sally Cantor bustled out from behind the counter with a rag and dustpan. "Don't you worry about it, Kaylee. I'll clean up the mess."

Jeremy returned with a glass of water, which he pressed into Kaylee's hands. I noticed one of her acrylic nails was missing.

"Drink some water, Kaylee. It will make you feel better."

"I may never feel better again," she said.

It sounded familiar to me, and I realized Magdalena Hillner had said something very similar to Pen Adams. Did either of the women really mean it? Seriously, Aaron may have been good-looking on the outside, but he was a class-A jerk on the inside. What was his appeal to these women?

She obediently took a gulp of the water and turned to look at me. "Please tell me I misunderstood what you said. Aaron can't be dead."

"I'm sorry, but he is. There was an ... um ... incident at the theater." I almost said accident, but until murder was ruled out, I thought incident was a better description.

"An incident? What kind of incident?"

Jeremy patted her shoulder and sat back down in his seat. "A piece of lighting equipment fell and struck him."

The young woman gasped, and her grip on the water glass slackened. I reached out and gently took it from her and put it on the table before Sally had to clean up another breakage.

"Then it was an accident. Miss Seldon said 'murder'

before. I heard her distinctly." Kaylee stared intently at Jeremy.

"Chief Carlow is looking into it, to determine exactly what happened," he said.

"I can't believe he's dead. And the last time I saw him was so awful. I wish I could turn back time."

"You mean last night at karaoke?" I asked.

She blinked at me owlishly. "No, after karaoke. I met him later. At the theater. He'd texted to say we had to talk."

"What did you talk about?" If my question seemed nosy, Kaylee didn't seem to notice, and she answered without pause.

"His wife coming into town and our relationship. He'd told me they were separated, but then she showed up, and I was so confused. Aaron explained they were separated in his heart."

Oh, brother. What a cock-and-bull line. Only a girl as young and naïve as Kaylee would fall for it. Jeremy and I exchanged a glance across the table, and I knew he was thinking the same thing.

"So you made up then?" Jeremy asked. "It doesn't sound like things ended too badly."

Kaylee's face flushed a shade of deep fuchsia. "While we were, y'know *making up*—"

I strongly suspected making out was closer to the truth than making up, but I merely nodded to encourage Kaylee to continue.

"My dad showed up at the theater. He'd seen my car turn in there on his way to pick up my little sister from a friend's house. He was not happy."

Finding his daughter in a compromising position with an older, very married man? I bet. "If it was my father, I suspect 'not happy' would be the understatement of the year."

She grimaced. "You're right. My dad was furious, and he fought with Aaron." Her pretty face crumpled, and she sniffed loudly as tears flooded her eyes. "But that wasn't the worst part. Aaron didn't stand up for our love. He just told Dad he understood, and he wouldn't see me again. Like I was nothing to him."

"How hurtful, Kaylee. I'm sorry," Jeremy said.

"I was hurt, but I was also furious. I mean, how could he throw our love away without a fight? When I asked him, he laughed and said he didn't love me. I was a summer fling. That was when I slapped him so hard I lost my nail."

I wanted to high-five her and say 'you go, girl' like I was on a daytime talk show, but with the man dead, it didn't seem appropriate, so I stayed quiet.

Kaylee took a long drink of water and looked at me. "I wish I could turn back time. So I'd never hit him. I'm sure if we spoke again, he would've explained he was just acting for my father's sake, and of course he loved me." A tear ran down her cheek. "Don't you think?"

I most certainly did not think it, but it seemed cruel to say so. "Maybe. I really didn't know him very well."

"Thank you both for talking to me. I'd better get home now." She stood and rushed out of the restaurant, chocking back a sob as she did.

"Looks like two more suspects, Kaylee and her father."

"Suspects?" Jeremy raised his eyebrows. "You're convinced it was murder then?"

"I have a hunch it is. Chief Carlow certainly seemed to think so, and he seems pretty savvy to me."

"Speaking of Danny, do you want to come back to the theater with me and see what's happening there?"

"Will they let us in?" I asked.

"Sure. I'm the manager. I have a right to check on the theater, doncha think?"

"I'm not completely convinced, but I think it sounds like an excellent excuse for us to get our sleuth on," I said as I grabbed my purse in one hand and my iced chai latte in the other.

"Where are you parked?" Jeremy asked as he stood.

"In the lot by the library."

"I'm on the street, so I'll meet you at the theater. Cara is going to be so jealous she's missing this Nancy Drew moment."

SINCE I HAD A LONGER WALK TO MY CAR, BY THE TIME I arrived at the theater, Jeremy was there and talking with a young police officer. Yellow caution tape was strung along the row of doors at the entrance. I juggled my keys, purse, and iced chai latte and shut the car door with my hip.

"I'm sorry I can't let you in, Mr. Patterson."

"I understand, Nicole. And I'm not your teacher anymore, you can call me Jeremy now."

I slung my purse over my shoulder and waved as I approached. "Hi. Sorry I took so long to get here."

"No worries, we can't go inside yet anyway, according to Officer Johnson. Nicole, this is my friend Amanda Seldon. She's working at the theater this summer too."

"Hi, Officer. Nice to meet you."

She looked at me with undisguised curiosity, and I remembered how fascinating it always was to see our teachers out in the wild. It always surprised me, as if they lived in stasis at the school when it wasn't in session. To find out they had friends, families, and a life outside the school had been amazing to me in my youth.

"Nice to meet you too, Ms. Seldon. Let me check inside to see when you both can get to your offices." She stepped away from us and pulled her radio from her belt. It crackled while she asked the chief about the status of the theater.

"Looks like we're not going to have our Nancy Drew moment after all," I said in a low voice and then took a sip of my drink.

Nicole stepped back to us. "The Chief said it's okay for you two to go into the lobby. He'd like to talk to you both. You can just duck under the tape."

"Thanks, Nicole." Jeremy gave her a jaunty salute with his coffee, and we headed for the entrance.

"The Chief wants to talk to us both? Does that sound ominous to you?" I asked, as I contorted myself and bobbled my beverage to duck under the yellow tape.

Jeremy followed with much more grace than me. "It does not. I think you've lived in a big city for too long. It's Danny Carlow. Dylan's big brother. You remember Dylan, right." He snickered. "To refresh your memory, in junior high you used to practice writing Mrs. Dylan Carlow in your notebooks."

I swung my purse at his leg, and he chuckled and deftly avoided the blow.

"Could we please not discuss such embarrassing memories in public? And for the record, I used to write Mrs. Amanda Seldon-Carlow. Not Mrs. Dylan Carlow."

"I stand corrected." Jeremy snorted.

Looking around the lobby, I noticed Magdalena Hillner seated on a bench with Pen Adams. I guess they hadn't been released yet. I jerked my head in their direction. "How do you think Magdalena got here this morning? There was no car here. And why is she in exercise gear? And Pen was pretty quick to arrive on the scene. Do you think there's some reason Chief Carlow isn't letting them leave?"

"You mean your brother-in-law?"

My only response was a glare.

"I don't know why Danny didn't let them leave. Only one way to find out, let's go over and ask them."

Chapter Six

"Hello, Pen. Magdalena." Jeremy managed to walk the line between friendly and somber.

"Jeremy, Amanda," Pen replied.

Magdalena looked me up and down. "You are very fashionable for a woman in this town in the middle of nowhere."

"Thank you." *I think.* I left the last bit unspoken in deference to Magdalena's recent loss, but seriously, what a catty comment.

"Amanda just moved back to Maple Hills. She's been living in Los Angeles for ten years, and before then, Manhattan."

"I worked in Manhattan." I corrected Jeremy. "I lived in Brooklyn. And it was before Brooklyn became hip. I could afford a better apartment there."

"You lived in Los Angeles until recently?" Magdalena straightened her spine and narrowed her eyes.

What was up with the hostility? In my previous position as VP of Human Resources, I frequently had to be an intermediary between different groups, so I'd developed diplomatic skills they'd be envious of at the United Nations. I pasted a smile to my face and nodded. "I did. I just got back here last week. But Maple Hills is my home-town. Why do you ask?"

"Aaron has been living in Los Angeles for a job. I had to stay in New York for my own work." She pursed her lips as she stared at me.

"It's a shame you had to be apart," I said, still not understanding her attitude. I guess grief can do funny things to people.

"It's interesting to me you had been in Los Angeles also."

"It's a big city. Lots of people there."

"True, but what I find intriguing is Aaron and you both arrived in Maple Hills last week. And now, here you are, working in the theater where he is directing a play. And when I arrived last night you were with Aaron in the bar. It is very coincidental. Don't you agree, Pen?"

The producer shrugged. "Like Amanda said, Los Angeles is a big city. And she was with her aunt last night at the tavern at another table, she'd just stopped by our table to introduce us to her aunt."

"But still, so many coincidences, and I don't like coinci-dences." Magdalena continued to glare at me.

I took a breath to defend my honor. I mean seriously, I was the only woman at the table not having an affair with her husband. Well, Aunt Lori and me. Although he was coming on to her pretty strong too. Before I could respond, a man's deep voice rumbled behind me.

"I don't like coincidences either, Mrs. Hillner. And unlike Mr. Adams, I agree there are too many coincidences there for my liking." Chief Carlow folded his arms across his broad chest. "Perhaps we could talk further in your office, Ms. Seldon."

He made it a statement, not a request, and I gulped. As the Chief strode off toward my office, I murmured to Jeremy, "Not ominous, huh? Shows what you know."

"Amanda's office is basically a closet with a desk and Wi-Fi. Why don't we go into mine?" Jeremy rushed ahead of Chief Carlow and threw open the door to his office, which was located across the lobby from mine.

The chief paused, and Jeremy winked at me as I scooted past him into his office, which truly was more spacious than mine. Jeremy entered behind me and took a seat behind his desk. As the chief entered, I sat in a guest seat across from my friend. I chose the one closest to the wall and regretted my decision when Chief Carlow sat in the one next to me and turned to stare at me. Well, not stare so much as examine. Like a cell under a microscope. Claustrophobia set in as I sat pinned between the chief and the wall. His eyebrows met in the middle of his face as he frowned at me.

"I assume, based on the widow's preposterous allegations about Amanda, you've determined Aaron's death was not an accident?" Jeremy asked.

His question mercifully took the chief's gaze off of me and onto Jeremy. "We are still investigating, but there is some preliminary evidence the rope was knotted loosely and sliced in a way to mimic fraying."

"In an attempt to disguise a murder as an accident?" I asked.

The glare was back on me now. When would I ever learn to keep my mouth shut?

"It is one possibility. Let's get back to you, Ms. Seldon. Did you know Aaron Hillner in Los Angeles?"

"I did not."

"Can you prove it?" He poked his index finger in my general direction.

"How do you prove you didn't know someone?" I held my hands out palms up, and they shook a little. Was the chief of police actually considering me as a murder suspect? "I can give you names and numbers of friends and coworkers back in LA, and they can tell you I didn't know Hillner—"

"Or they can tell me they didn't know you knew Hillner, which is not at all the same thing," Chief Carlow interrupted.

"And we've circled back to my original point. How do I prove I didn't know him?"

"It just seems suspicious to me you were both living in Los Angeles right before you arrived in Maple Hills within a week of each other. Quite a coincidence, in fact." He scowled at me.

"Los Angeles is not Maple Hills. Almost four million people live there. I didn't work in the entertainment industry and didn't hang out with a theater crowd. I worked in human resources. It would have been miraculous if I had met Hillner there."

"Danny, you know I respect you and your position, but you're barking up the wrong tree here." Jeremy raked his hands through his hair.

"Then help me by proving she did not have a relationship with Aaron Hillner before they both came to Maple Hills. Heck, Jeremy, I don't want to believe this about one of your buddies. You're friends with my brother."

I turned my head so fast to stare at Jeremy my neck cracked. He was friends with my childhood crush? This was new information. Why had he never mentioned Dylan to me?

Jeremy held up one finger to forestall my unspoken question and turned back to Danny Carlow. "We'll get you the names and numbers Amanda offered. You can check with the people she knew in Los Angeles. Maybe coordinate with the police there to try to track her movements in the weeks before she moved. But I can tell you right now, the end result is you will learn Amanda never met Hillner before she came to Maple Hills. I think your time would be better served by looking into other possible motives a little closer to home."

"Like who?" Carlow asked.

"Kaylee Tufton, for one. Did you know she actually was carrying on an affair with Hillner?"

The chief fell back in his chair. "I did not. She's a lot younger than him and has a boyfriend. How do you know this information? Is it from a reliable source?"

"The horse's mouth. Kaylee told us this morning," Jeremy said. "She also said her father caught them in a compromising position last night and was furious. There are two far more likely suspects for you."

"I can't believe little Kaylee or Larry Tufton would be capable of murder."

Jeremy pursed his lips. "Really? If you found out a man like Aaron Hillner was romantically involved with one of your daughters, you'd be fine with it?"

Carlow ran his hand over his jaw and shook his head. "Of course not."

"And the lead actress in the play dedicated a really romantic song to Aaron at karaoke night yesterday at the Hitchcock Tavern. What's her name?" I looked at Jeremy for assistance.

"Maisy Lapointe. It was an open secret around the theater Aaron and she were having an affair," Jeremy said.

"And what about Melville Dickens? I ran into him at

the library this morning when I was visiting my Aunt Lori, and he was irate about what Hillner had done to his novel. He called it an abomination. He's staying at the Dew Drop Inn if you want to talk to him."

"There are four people right there who are more likely suspects than Amanda. A person who had no connection to Aaron Hillner until yesterday, in spite of what his wife and you seem to think," Jeremy said.

"You've given me plenty to think about." The chief looked between Jeremy and me. "But I'll still need those names and numbers in Los Angeles. And I'd like to look at your fingernails, Amanda."

I held out my hands for his inspection. "My fingernails? Why?"

He peered at my hands. "You don't have acrylic nails."

"No. I was always too busy with work to keep up a manicure. I just keep them short and unpolished." Fifty and sixty hour work weeks didn't leave a lot of time for pampering.

"You didn't answer her question, Danny. Why do you want to see Amanda's nails?" Jeremy asked with a frown.

"Just between us, we found an acrylic nail on the stage."

"A long, sort of beige-colored one?" I asked.

Chief Carlow's eyes bugged. "Yes, how did you know?"

"Because Kaylee slapped him so hard one of hers popped off last night. I bet it was hers," I said.

He took a deep breath and exhaled slowly. "The theater is yours again, Jeremy. We'll still be around working on our investigation, but you can resume your normal routine here. I told the play's producer too. And now, I need to get a move on, it looks like I have a lot of work to do. We need to call your friends in Los Angeles, and I need to talk to Kaylee."

At least the chief was willing to consider other suspects, but as long as I was still on the list, our Nancy Drew moment wasn't over. I needed to do whatever I could to find the real killer and clear my name.

WHEN THE POLICE CHIEF LEFT WITH THE CONTACT information for my nearest and dearest in LA, I swung my gaze to my best friend. "You're friends with Dylan Carlow? Since when?"

Jeremy straightened some papers on the desk and pointedly avoided eye contact. That was the thing about knowing each other since we were kids. We knew all of each other's tells. And Jeremy's behavior right now was screaming at me there was plenty he wasn't telling me.

"A few years. He's the assistant swim coach at the high school, so we've gotten to know each other at work. They wanted him to be the coach, but the orchard keeps him busy, so they compromised. Anyway, he's a good guy."

"So you're work friends?" I sensed a mystery here, and it wasn't Hillner's murder.

Jeremy moved on to checking his phone. "Mm-hmm. And we hang out sometimes. Like I said, he's a good guy."

"Does Cara know?"

"Sure. She's friendly with him too."

"And neither of my two oldest friends in the whole world thought I might be interested in the information they were hanging out..." I put air quotes around the last two words. "...with the person I had a mad crush on from age eleven to eighteen?"

"Do I know the names of every person you've gone out for drinks with after work since you've moved to LA? No, I don't."

"And I felt like the chief didn't like me for some reason when we met. Before I was his prime murder suspect. He acted like he knew who I was, but he was years ahead of us in school. By the time we were in high school, he was in college."

"Danny is protective of Dylan. Even though they're both grown men now, he has a serious big-brother complex."

"And Dylan needs to be protected from me? He never even knew I was alive."

Jeremy's phone pinged, and he ignored me as he read. "Speak of the devil. It's from Danny. He says he's releasing the theater, although the police will still be in and out as they investigate."

"But—"

His phone pinged again, and Jeremy cut off my impending question about the Dylan Carlow friendship mystery. "And I just got one from Pen. Since everyone has arrived for their one o'clock rehearsal, they're going to have a meeting of the cast and crew in the theater right now. What do you say we sit in the back and listen. I for one am curious about what Aaron's death means for the production."

I screwed up my mouth and huffed out a breath through my nose. "Fine. I am curious. But this discussion about the Carlow brothers is not over."

WE DUCKED INTO THE THEATER AND SLID INTO THE TWO seats right by the door in the back.

Pen Adams stood in front of the stage and addressed the assembled cast and crew. I scanned the group for Magdalena Hillner and didn't see her. She must've left, even though she was a coproducer with Pen. I guess it made sense. The murdered man was her husband after all, and even if their marriage had been less than ideal from my perspective, she must be mourning his loss.

"So that's where we stand," Pen said. "The police will still need to talk to us, and I expect everyone to cooperate fully. We cannot leave town. I've discussed the matter with Mrs. Hillner, and we've decided since we are stuck here for the time being, while they investigate Aaron's death, we should go ahead with our production of *Ecstasy in the Aspens*. Magdalena suggested we dedicate these performances to Aaron."

A sob sounded from the first row, and I craned my neck to see who it was. Maisy Lapointe. One of Aaron's apparently many women. In spite of the fact he had a wife and another girlfriend here in Maple Hills, and goodness only knew how many in LA and New York, it seemed Maisy was truly grief-stricken by his death. Or had she killed him and this was all a big show? The woman was an actress after all.

Pen raised his voice to be heard above her wails. "I know we all cared about Aaron—"

A general titter and hum of whispered remarks met his statement. Looked like most of the cast and crew did not, in fact, care about Aaron.

He continued as if no one had spoken. "—but he was a pro and he would've wanted the show to go on, so it shall. I'll step in as director until we can find a replacement. Let's all work together to make *Ecstasy* a roaring success as a way to honor Aaron's memory."

His rousing conclusion was met with silence. Well, except for Maisy who had stopped sobbing and merely snuffled loudly now. A smattering of half-hearted applause broke out among the crowd, and several people stood up to leave.

"No!" A deep voice bellowed from the center of the crowd.

"Can you see who's yelling?" Jeremy whispered.

"Melville Dickens," I replied in a low voice. Although I don't know why I bothered. No one could hear me while the author bellowed his rant at top volume and everyone froze in place and watched him.

He stood up and shoved people out of the way to get to Pen, as his tirade continued. "I cannot pretend to mourn this man. He was a murderer himself."

"I say, that's a strong accusation," Pen said. "Who do you think Aaron killed?"

"He was a murderer of literature," Melville said. "His production has made a mockery of my work, and I'd hoped his death would mean an end of this theatrical farce."

Jeremy and I exchanged a glance.

He leaned in and whispered, "Do you think Melville Dickens killed Aaron in the hopes it would put a stop to this play?"

"I don't know. But if he did, he killed Aaron for nothing because the show is going on."

Chapter Seven

I pulled into the parking lot by the town sporting fields. As the Three Musketeers were not especially sporty, this was not a place I spent a lot of time as a kid. But Cara's children were athletic, and she'd invited Jeremy and me to come and watch her son Martin's Little League game. Luckily, dogs were allowed at the park because Fluffy had been indignant when I got home after the meeting at the theater.

If you don't think a shih tzu can look thoroughly ticked off, then you've never known one. But after I took her out, and maybe bribed her with a treat or two, Fluffy and I were once again besties. I attached her leash and let her out of the car, and we followed the sound of cheering and the thwonk of a bat hitting a ball.

The fields looked a little more polished than when I'd last been here. I distinctly remember having to bring a blanket and sit on the ground if you wanted to watch a game. Now there were metal stands for spectators.

Fluffy trotted obediently at my side, her plumed tail waving above her back like a flag.

"Amanda, over here!"

I looked toward the sound of Cara's voice and saw her in the front row of the stands waving both arms above her head. I waved back and picked up Fluffy. She was fine over here with just the two of us, but the crowd might trigger anxiety for her, and when she got worked up, there was always a chance she could snap out of fear. My girl had issues, I'm not gonna lie. But I loved her to pieces.

Jeremy and Cara scooted over on the aluminum bench seat to make room for me. I sat, and held Fluffy on my lap. She promptly turned to Jeremy and bared her teeth. A growl rumbled low in her throat. I stroked her head in a soothing, rhythmic manner.

"Hi, guys. Thanks for saving me a seat. This is a lot fancier than it used to be." I squinted into the sun at the baseball diamond. "Where's Martin?"

Cara pointed at the boy currently warming up with a bat. "You're just in time. He's up next."

I looked over at Martin and noticed the man standing next to him. He was tall, with broad shoulders and a narrow waist. His hair was brown, but the sun glinting off of it revealed streaks of blond and auburn. The light formed a halo around his head, and I may have heard the angels sing. Because it was none other than Dylan Carlow, my childhood crush.

I swiped my palms on my white denim capri pants. All the moisture from my mouth seemed to have gone straight to my hands, as it was currently as dry as the Sahara. Seriously, nomads were getting ready to set up camp in there.

"Is that Dylan Carlow next to Martin?" my voice rasped, and I cleared my throat.

Cara reached in a huge, striped tote bag by her side and pulled out a bottle of water, which she handed to me. "Sure is. He's filling in as coach today."

"How does he manage to look even more handsome now than when he was eighteen?"

Jeremy studied Dylan through narrowed eyes, and then turned to inspect Cara and me. "I think we all look better than we did then."

"I agree, but Dylan is definitely a hottie. All the moms love it when he comes to the games," Cara said.

As Martin stepped up to bat, she put her hands around her mouth and hooted. "Go, Martin! You got this."

Jeremy clapped loudly and since my hands were full of nervous dog and a water bottle, I settled for cheering loudly. "Yay, Martin! Show them what's what."

Cara glanced away from her son briefly to look at me. "Show them what's what? You have seriously got to work on your cheering if we're going to spend a summer watching these games together."

At my goofy words, Dylan looked my way, and his eyes widened. He waved, and I looked over my shoulder to see who was behind me. He laughed and shook his head and pointed at me and waved again.

"The mom brigade is going to be so jealous." Jeremy whistled low between his teeth.

I feared my cheeks were as red as the team jerseys. "Is he waving at me?"

"Looks like," Cara said. "Now could we please save the soap opera talk until my son bats?"

I mimed zipping my lips, and put all my attention on the game. I could figure out how Dylan Carlow even knew I was alive later.

～

THE GAME ENDED WITH A VICTORY FOR THE MAPLE HILLS Vikings. As soon as the game was over, Dylan headed for us like a real Viking headed for Greenland.

Jeremy waved and called out, "Hi, Dylan."

He smiled as he approached, and his teeth were so white, I'm surprised toothpaste companies weren't lined up to have him as their spokesmodel. "If it isn't the Three Musketeers, together again."

My heart thudded in my chest, and suddenly I was seventeen again.

"Great game, Dylan. Thanks for filling in for Danny today," Cara said.

"Martin did good," he said with a grin and a cheery head bob.

"You remember—" Jeremy began, but was interrupted by Dylan.

"Amanda Seldon. I sure do. Welcome back to Maple Hills." His eyes crinkled at the corners when he smiled at me.

Up close, I could see he did actually look his age, but I stood by my belief he was even more handsome. His skin was golden from the sun, and slightly weathered, probably from working at the family's orchard.

My mouth went dry again, and I unscrewed the top of the water bottle to take a sip. Cara slipped her foot to the side and her sandal made contact with my ankle. She smiled at Dylan all the while, but hissed between her teeth to me, "Speak."

Right. Speak. The thing normal humans did when someone addressed them. "Hi, Dylan."

Ah, banter worthy of Noel Coward. What was wrong with me? Usually I was more poised with people. My previous job kind of depended on it.

"Good game today, man." Jeremy spoke and saved my bacon.

"The kids played well. I'm glad we got the 'W', I would've really hated to report back to Danny that they'd lost with me at the helm. He was too busy at work to come today."

Right. His brother was too busy calling my friends in LA to see if I was lying about knowing Aaron Hillner to fulfill his coaching duties.

Fluffy strained to break free of my grasp, and I put her down on the ground next to where I sat on the bottom row of the stands. She surprised me by wagging her tail and trotting toward Dylan.

His face lit up at the sight of the adorable little dog, and he squatted down and held out his hand. "Hey there, girl. What's your name?"

My heart pounded. "Don't do that!" Fluffy had been known to fake someone out by looking darling and then bite them while their guard was down.

"Do what?" Dylan asked as Fluffy tentatively sniffed his extended hand and then graciously allowed him to pet her.

"I was afraid she'd snap at you." Since the leash was stretched between us, I stood up and walked closer to Fluffy, which put me in scent range of Dylan. He smelled like clean laundry that had been hung on the line, with a little hint of citrusy cologne. I melted inside as I inhaled.

"This sweetheart snap at me? No way, would you, girl?"

"The Beast most decidedly could and would snap at you. Her behavior right now is some kind of canine miracle," Jeremy said.

Dylan squinted up at me. "Her name is The Beast?"

I swung my gaze to glare at Jeremy. "It is not. Her name is Fluffy. Jeremy just fancies himself a comedian."

"Okay, gotcha," Dylan said in a way that left no doubt he had no idea what we were talking about. He stood up and said, "I have to wrap things up with the team, but after would you guys like to grab some dinner?"

I was grateful for my big, round sunglasses, as they covered up my eyes which had widened to cartoon-like proportions behind them. I forced myself to blink and breathe.

Cara answered quickly. Too quickly. "I can't. Once Martin is ready, we need to go pick up his sister from a friend's house."

She swatted Jeremy in a none-too-subtle manner. He rubbed his arm and said, "Sorry, buddy. Eric is waiting for me at home. He made a special dinner for us. Enchiladas. My favorite."

I narrowed my eyes at Jeremy. The level of detail in his excuse was definitely overplaying his hand.

"Amanda? How about you? Us single folks have to stick together, right?" He scuffed the toe of one sneaker on the dirt. "You are single still, right?"

Was Dylan Carlow seriously asking me my relation-ship status? And out to dinner? I stood like a statue, until Cara swatted my arm, and I learned why Jeremy had rubbed his. It hurt. She packed quite a wallop for a tiny woman.

Fluffy growled at her for daring to lay her hand on me.

Jeremy pointed at my dog. "See what I mean. The Beast."

"That sounds good," I suddenly found my voice.

"Calling her The Beast?" Dylan asked.

"No. Dinner. I meant dinner sounds good."

"Great. I need to finish up with the kids. Can you give

me about an hour? Then maybe we could grab something at the diner. I'm not really dressed for anything nicer."

"The diner is perfect. I'll run Fluffy home and feed her and then meet you there in an hour."

"Coach Carlow, what should we do with the snacks?" one of the boys yelled.

"Gotta run. See you at the diner." He jogged backwards a couple of steps while he beamed at me, and then turned to trot over to the team.

"You've got a date with Dylan," Jeremy said in a singsong voice.

My heart pounded in my chest. I did have a date with Dylan Carlow. It almost made up for being a murder suspect.

THE THREE OF US WALKED TO THE PARKING LOT TOGETHER, Martin would meet Cara at their SUV once the post-game team meeting was over.

"So ... a date with Dylan Carlow. Better late than never." Cara winked at me, as she hoisted her tote bag into the hatch of her vehicle.

A slight sheen of sweat formed at my hairline, and my heart thumped. "It's not a date. He asked all of us to go, I was just the only one who could."

"It seems date-like to me." Jeremy bobbed his head.

A young man I recognized from the game as being the assistant coach trotted across the parking lot toward us. "Mr. Patterson, hold up for a minute."

"Sure thing, Caleb." Jeremy leaned into me and spoke quietly. "Caleb Symansky. He's Kaylee Tufton's boyfriend."

"I wonder what he wants with you?" I asked.

Jeremy shrugged as the young man reached us. He was long and lean with short brown hair and dressed in the team tee shirt, the bright red of a maple leaf in autumn with a cartoon of a Viking in the middle.

"Thanks for waiting, sir."

I'll never get used to Jeremy being the teacher and sir worthy to his students. To me, he would forever be the goofy boy who used to crouch behind my parents log pile with me and pretend we were in a cabin.

"No problem, Caleb. What's up?"

The young man hesitated and slanted a nervous gaze at Cara and me. He swallowed hard and spoke. "I wanted to talk to you about the play."

"The play?" Jeremy cocked his head. "What about the play?"

"I heard a rumor it's going to continue, even without that Hillner guy. As a sort of tribute to him, even." His face looked like thunder.

"It's what the producers have decided, yes," Jeremy said.

"How can you let it happen? A tribute to a married man who would mess around with a girl young enough to be his daughter."

Ah, there's the rub. Caleb knew about his girlfriend and the director. And based on his clenched fists and bright red spots on his cheeks, he was not happy about it.

Cara wrinkled her nose. "I'd seen Hillner around town. Was he really old enough to be Kaylee's father? I mean he was hot."

Caleb spun in her direction. "Hot? He was a filthy pig." Spittle might have flown from his lips.

"I'm sorry, Caleb. I know you're hurt, but he was a good looking man." Cara took a step back, probably to get out of saliva range.

"On the outside," I amended. "You never met him, but on the inside it seemed like he was kind of a jerk."

Caleb waved his hands at me. "Thank you."

"Whatever we all think about Hillner, the show is going on, and I'm sorry but it's not my call." Jeremy reached out and squeezed the young man's shoulder. "I think you shouldn't worry about it too much. I know you're angry with Kaylee right now—"

"I'm not angry," Caleb interrupted. "Well maybe I am, but mostly I'm hurt."

"I know, buddy. But above all else, you care for Kaylee, and she's going through something really difficult right now. Can you be there for her as a friend?" Jeremy spoke in a low, soothing voice.

Caleb's shoulders slumped. "I want to, but she's not taking my calls. And according to Destiny," he turned to look at me and explained, "Destiny is my sister; she's Kaylee's best friend."

I smiled at him and nodded for him to continue.

"According to Destiny, Kaylee still wants to volunteer at the theater as a way to honor his memory. She knows he was married, and even seeing other women on the side too, but she still claims to love him and want to honor him. I was hoping maybe you could shut down the show. I'm sure if she just had a little distance from it, she'd realize what a creep he was and remember what we had together."

Poor kid. I know he was twenty-one, so technically an adult, but at his age, emotions were still so raw and all-encompassing.

"It's out of my hands, Caleb. I just manage the theater, and if the production team wants the show to go on, then it will."

"You could stop Kaylee from volunteering." Caleb jutted out his chin.

"But I won't. She needs to work through all this in her own way. Trying to stop her from working at the theater won't help and quite frankly seems a little controlling," Jeremy's voice was still understanding, but had a hint of steel to it now.

"Maybe it is, but if the end result is we get back together, then I don't care." Caleb shouted and turned to run back to the field.

"That boy is one giant ball of jealousy, anger, and pain. I'm not looking forward to my kids hitting the teen years," Cara said.

"I'm wondering if his jealousy, anger, and pain are strong enough he might've decided to take control over the situation and end Aaron Hillner's life," I said. "I think we need to look into where Caleb was when Hillner was murdered."

"Good idea," Cara said.

"But first you need to get home, drop off The Beast, and maybe freshen up your hair and makeup before your date with Dylan," Jeremy said.

"It's not a date," I protested. But my friends only laughed.

"Text me later to let me know how it went," Cara said as Martin approached.

"And please consider the hair and makeup suggestion," Jeremy called over his shoulder as he walked toward his car.

Lifelong friends. You had to love them.

Chapter Eight

I fed Fluffy, took her out, and ran a brush through my hair in record time, so as not to be late for my not-date with Dylan. My car squealed to a stop in the first open space I saw in the parking lot for the Sunny Side Up Diner, more commonly known just as the Diner, or sometimes Sunny's. Sunny Baker was the owner of the diner and had been since I was a kid.

I paused long enough to glide some peachy-colored gloss on my lips and hopped out of the car. Punctuality was kind of my thing. It stood me in good stead in the business world, but to be honest, ever since I can remember, if I wasn't at least five minutes early, I considered myself late.

When I entered the diner, Sunny herself was working as hostess. Her hair was still styled in the same bleached and teased-within-an-inch-of-its-life style she'd had for as long as I'd known her.

Her face lit up when she saw me enter. "Amanda Seldon, I'm so happy you're back in Maple Hills."

She came out from behind the cash register and enveloped me in a hug, and the powdery scent of her perfume mixed with the delectable aroma of bacon took me right back to childhood.

"It's good to see you, Mrs. Baker." I closed my eyes and squeezed her in return.

"Sunny, for goodness sake. I think you're old enough to call me by my first name now." She chuckled as she pulled away from me and grabbed a menu off the counter. "Table for one? Or are you meeting the other two Musketeers?"

A deep voice rumbled behind me. "Actually, she's meeting me."

I turned around and saw Dylan stand from the first booth next to the window.

There was a speculative gleam in Sunny's eyes as she looked between us. "Isn't this an interesting development."

She led me to the red vinyl booth, and Dylan took a couple of steps to meet us in the middle.

"Sorry I'm late," I blurted out as heat flooded my cheeks. I really did hate being late, and I wanted to impress Dylan, even after all these years.

"You're not late. I was early. It's kind of a problem with me. If I'm not early, I feel

like—"

"—I'm late," We both spoke at once.

"Such nice kids. You were always two of my favorites. It's nice to see you together," Sunny said as she slapped my giant, faux leather-bound menu on the table and strolled back to the hostess stand.

I slid into the booth, and Dylan did the same across from me.

"I met your brother this morning," I said as I opened the menu and perused it.

He winced as he did the same. "I heard."

"Then you heard he thinks I'm a murderer."

"I'm sure he doesn't really think it," Dylan said.

"I'm pretty sure he does, but I guess I understand he has to follow every lead. Let's talk about something else. He told me you're running the family orchard now."

Dylan smiled, and I swear the sun outside shone a little brighter. One of the things I crushed on him about back in the day was his cheerful, good nature. I tended toward being a glass-half-empty kind of person, but his glass always seemed to be half-full.

"I studied business and agriculture at UConn, and came back to work here with my dad after graduation. My folks decided to retire early a couple of years ago, and I took over the operation. I love it. It's what I always dreamed about doing. Jeremy tells me you're back in town to do what you've always dreamed of doing too."

My smile faltered a bit around the edges. Jeremy better have been talking about my writing and not Dylan. "Yep. I'm here to finally give being an author a shot. I'm really excited about it. Human resources could be rewarding, but it was a serious grind, so I'm excited to step back from it and begin my first novel."

He put his menu down and rested his elbows on the table to lean in to me. "I'm a huge reader. What are you writing?"

I closed my menu too. I don't know why I was looking; I always get the same thing at Sunny's. "It's historical fiction. A mystery, set in Boston at the turn of the last century—"

"Ready to order?" A waitress interrupted with her pen and pad at the ready.

"I am, because I almost always get the same thing here for lunch or dinner. Are you, Amanda?"

"Me too."

"I'd like a turkey club." We both spoke at once, and then laughed.

"On whole wheat toast," we continued in unison.

"You two are really in sync. What can I get you to drink?" the waitress asked.

"A diet cola," I said.

"Here's where our orders diverge. I'd like an iced tea please. With lemon."

"Coming right up," the waitress called over her shoulder as she walked away from our booth.

"The waitress spared you a long-winded monologue about what I'm writing. I'm actually still at the research stage now, but I could talk about it for hours."

"I want to hear about it. Like I said, I love to read, and mysteries are one of my favorite genres. Tell me all about it."

He asked for it.

WE'D FINISHED OUR IDENTICAL SANDWICHES, AND ORDERED coffee, with a piece of lemon meringue pie for Dylan. I couldn't eat another bite.

"My mom would say we've solved all the problems of the world tonight, we talked so much," Dylan said with a chuckle.

The conversation between us flowed like water. We had a surprising number of interests in common, and a similar sense of humor. It really was one of the nicest date ... er... *non*-dates I've had in a while. Maybe ever. And as a special bonus, Dylan didn't seem to share his brother's opinion about me being some sort of bloodthirsty killer.

An older woman with a tight perm walked by our table and stopped short, her jaw dropped. "As I live and breathe, it's Amanda Seldon. Good to see you." The familiar voice still had the rasp of a pack-a-day smoker, although I knew the lady had kicked the habit two decades before.

I jumped up to hug her. "Mrs. Godfrey, hello!"

"Call me Carol. I'm not your boss anymore." She winked at Dylan and jerked her thumb at me. "This one worked for me at the Dew Drop the summer she turned sixteen. She was a hard worker, but one of the worst chamber maids I ever had."

I threw back my head and laughed, not at all insulted.

"I can't believe it," Dylan leapt staunchly to my defense.

"It's true," I said. "I stunk."

"And so did the rooms after you doused them in cleaning product. P. U." Carol pinched the end of her nose.

"I wanted to make sure they were good and sanitized," I said.

"They were. You used enough bleach the doc could've performed surgery in our guest rooms the summer you worked at the Dew Drop."

The waitress came up with our coffees.

"Would you care to join us?" Dylan asked.

"We're finished eating, but I would love the chance to catch up with you," I said.

"Nope. I'm meeting the girls here tonight. We get together once a week for dinner, whether we want to or not." Carol laughed at her own joke. "I'm the first one here tonight."

"Then keep us company until they get here," Dylan said.

I sat back down and scooted over to make room for my old boss.

"Don't mind if I do," Carol said.

"I met one of your guests. Melville Dickens," I said.

She scrunched up her face. "That one is a piece of work. He got hit hard by the whack-a-doodle stick."

I added a packet of sugar substitute and some creamer to my coffee. The spoon clinked against the sturdy, white porcelain mug as I stirred. "He is different."

"He mostly keeps to himself, so I can't complain too much. Last night I don't know if he even stayed in his room."

"Really?" I asked and took a sip of my coffee.

"He drives this beat-up old jalopy. Last night I couldn't sleep. I have trouble with insomnia since I hit menopause. Anyhoo, I was wide awake at one o'clock, and I looked out the window, and his car wasn't in the lot. Weren't there again this morning when I walked over to the office."

Carol lived in a small cottage on the grounds of her motel, and she never missed a trick. Seemed like some things never changed.

I tried to not seem too interested in Dickens's movements, but it sounded like his story about where he was during the time frame of Aaron's murder was a bunch of hooey. "When was the last time you saw his car?"

She screwed up her mouth and took a moment before she answered. "Sometime yesterday morning, I'd say." She snapped her fingers. "Wait a minute, no. I saw it again in the afternoon, but it was gone by the time *Jeopardy* came on television."

"So not after seven o'clock last night?" I probed.

"Not unless he popped back and I missed it." She shook her head.

And we all knew Carol missing a trick at the Dew Drop was about as likely as Fluffy winning Miss Congeniality at a dog show.

A loud chorus of voices sounded from the front door and Carol turned sideways in the booth to look. "The girls are here. It was good seeing you, Amanda. Stop by the next time you're out by the lake. We can have a good old chin wag."

"Will do, Carol."

I turned back to face straight ahead and saw Dylan studying me through narrowed eyes.

"What? Do I have something on my face?" I dabbed around my mouth with my napkin.

"No, you look perfect."

My heart thumped at his observation, until it stopped at his next words.

"It looked to me like you were trying to break that guy's alibi. He's part of the theater production, right? Jeremy told me about him. He's quite a character, evidently."

I sat up straight. "It doesn't sound to me like he has an alibi at all."

"My brother is good at his job. He'll get to the bottom of what happened."

"I'm sure he is, but as long as I'm his prime suspect, he's not looking at the right person. Because I know I'm innocent. So, I'm going to do everything in my power to find the real murderer."

"You're playing a dangerous game, Amanda. If you insist on pursuing someone who's already killed once, please promise me you'll be careful."

"Careful is my middle name," I said, but my voice quavered a bit.

I always was the type of person to consider all the options and proceed with caution, but less than a week back in Maple Hills and suddenly I was hunting down a killer. I swiped my suddenly sweaty palms on the napkin in my lap. What the heck was I thinking?

THE NEXT MORNING, I HIT THE THEATER BRIGHT AND EARLY in the hope of getting some research done for my book before Jeremy arrived for work. Once he got there, I knew the interrogation about my dinner with Dylan would begin in earnest.

I got Fluffy settled on her little dog bed in my postage stamp-sized office, shut the door, and opened my laptop. My plan was successful for about two hours.

Lost in a website on early twentieth-century New England, I started when a rap sounded on my door. Fluffy jumped up and barked ferociously.

"I know you're in there, Amanda. Your car's in the lot. Contain The Beast and spill all the tea about last night."

"Come on in, Jeremy." I bent over, picked up Fluffy, and held her on my lap.

The door opened a crack, and he peeked in. "I assume since the barking stopped you have your little monster under control?"

"She's on my lap, you big chicken. Come in."

He entered and plopped on the wooden chair across the small desk from me. "Tell me everything. No detail is too small."

"We met at the diner. I got to see Sunny. Oh, and Carol Godfrey was there too, which was fun—"

"Stop." He held up one hand like a traffic cop and shut his eyes. "While it is thrilling you met with Sunny and Carol, really it is, I want to hear about Dylan and you."

"We had a nice time. We have more in common than I would've expected, and the conversation flowed. It was fun."

"Are you seeing each other again? Did he kiss you?"

"It's Maple Hills, Jer. With a population of roughly

three thousand people, I think it's safe to say we'll be seeing each other again. And, no, we didn't kiss. It wasn't a date."

"Bah. That's no fun."

"It was fun though. Really. He was nice, and funny, and smart. We had a good time. What did you expect to happen? We'd launch into a passionate affair? Dylan isn't Aaron Hillner. He's not that kind of guy."

"You're right. He is one of the good ones. Unlike Hillner, not to speak ill of the dead or anything. Although, now we're talking about him, I had a thought about his murder."

Since Fluffy had calmed down, I placed her back on her dog bed. Jeremy watched me with narrowed eyes. "Are you sure that's safe?"

"Yes. Just shut the door behind you please."

The room was small enough Jeremy was able to close it without standing up, he just reached behind him and swung it shut.

I leaned my forearms on the desk. "So what's your thought about the murder?"

"If someone cut the rope to make it look like an accident, the killer had to have been up in the rafters. Someone with knowledge of the theater."

"Hmm ... like a crew member?" I suggested.

"It seems likely. And from what I've heard around the theater, Aaron wasn't popular with them."

I snorted. "He wasn't popular with anyone, except apparently a sub-group of the female population."

"He was pretty."

"On the outside," I corrected. "Were any of the crew members angrier at him than the others?"

"Not that I know of, but I can ask around today. You know how gossipy theater folks are. Especially a travelling troupe like this one. They've been touring with this show for a few months now, and are like a dysfunctional family at this point. I'm sure I can find out more from them if I turn on the old Patterson charm."

"Sounds like a plan." I paused. "Quite possibly a *flawed* plan, if it all hinges on your ability to charm."

He picked up a pen from my desk and tossed it in my general direction. I easily dodged it, but it landed on the ground next to Fluffy, who stood up and growled at it.

"Your brave defender," Jeremy said with a dramatic eye roll.

"She is." I stood up for my girl.

"What's your plan for the day?"

"I'm just wrapping up my research, and I'm going to contact the volunteers. I'm afraid some of the kids won't want to work here anymore, what with the murder and all."

"Good idea, although I would bet money the kids will still be all in; it's their parents who might not want their little darlings volunteering at a murder scene."

"True. Either way, we need to learn who's still working and who's not. Then afterwards, I'm going to Cara's for lunch. Do you want to come with? I'm sure she wouldn't mind. You guys could double-team me about Dylan."

"Tempting as it sounds, I don't think so, but thanks. I've got a lot of work to do, on top of my snooping around the crew looking for suspects. Do you have any plans of a sleuthing nature?"

I nodded. "Carol Godfrey told me last night Melville Dickens's car was not at the motel in the wee hours the night of the murder. I'd like to poke around a little to see what I can learn about where he was."

"Be careful you don't poke a hornet's nest. Melville doesn't strike me as the most stable person, and if he's the killer and realizes you're on to him, you might be putting yourself in danger."

"I'll be careful." I crossed my heart.

But after Jeremy left my office, my heart pounded in my chest. He had a point. We all needed to be careful as we searched for the real killer. If they had killed once, what would stop them from killing again if they felt threatened?

Chapter Nine

Cara and I sat in the shade of an umbrella at a round table by her pool. The hum of the pool motor in the shed and bird song were the only sounds.

"Where are the kids?"

"Martin has baseball practice, and Charlotte is at the lake for morning camp, and then she has swimming practice at the Y. She's on the Maple Hills Minnows. Dylan coaches the team."

"Dylan told me about coaching the Minnows last night. But I didn't realize Charlotte was on the team. Your kids are so much sportier than we were." I took a sip of my fizzy water and eyed the delectable salad in the middle of the table. My mouth may have watered just the teensiest bit at the sight of the mixed greens tossed with fresh berries, walnuts, and chunks of creamy blue cheese.

Cara must have seen the gleam in my eye, as she passed the salad bowl and tongs to me. "Dig in, but then I want to hear all about your not-date with Dylan. And for you to catch me up on the investigation into the play director's death. What was his name again?"

I served myself a heaping portion of the salad and reached for a slice of the warm, crusty bread. Which I promptly slathered with butter. So much for the healthy salad. "Aaron Hillner. And there's a lot to tell."

We ate, and I filled Cara in on everything that was happening.

She chewed in a thoughtful manner, swallowed, and said, "Do you think it's the author? It seems shady he was out all night. Unless he was having a romantic rendezvous?"

"Melville Dickens doesn't come across like the romantic rendezvous type. He's laser focused on his work, and what Hillner has done with his book."

Cara wrinkled her nose. "Is the script adaptation really the director's call? Or would it be the producer's?"

"I'm not sure. We'd have to ask Jeremy." My phone pinged from the table next to me, and I picked it up to look. "Speak of the devil. It's Jeremy. He said he's talked to the crew. And they told him it doesn't have to be someone with knowledge of the theater to drop the light. Since it's a hemp house theater, it could be someone with a knowledge of sailing."

"Sailing?" Cara asked.

My phone pinged again. "More from Jeremy. It's like he heard our question. He said in early theater, sailors used to frequently be employed as stage hands, because of their knowledge of knots. They were excellent at rigging the theater equipment, in the same way they would rig the sails. Interesting."

"Wait a minute. Are you saying Jeremy talked to the crew about them being the only ones with the skills to commit the murder? And they just answered him? Without being insulted?"

I shrugged as my thumbs tapped on my phone. "I'll ask him."

While we waited for his response, Cara said, "Do we know if any of the suspects have sailing experience?"

"No. But I'll add it to my list of things to check. Which is growing by the minute." My phone pinged, and I chuckled and shook my head as I read the message to Cara. "Jeremy says it's because he's so charming."

"And humble," Cara added with a snort.

Her phone played a snippet of a song. "That's Charlotte's ring tone. Hang on." She picked up her phone and read it. "I'm sorry. I need to pick her up at camp and bring her to swim practice. I know people joke about it, but I didn't realize how much of motherhood would be chauffeuring my kids around town. Do you want to come for a ride?"

"Sure. I'll help you bring this stuff inside." I stood and picked up my plate and the bread basket. "It will be nice to take a spin down by the lake. But then I have to get sleuthing."

I SANK INTO THE PLUSH, LEATHER UPHOLSTERY OF CARA'S luxury SUV. "Are these seats cooled?"

"Yep. When you spend as much time as I do in this rig, you learn to splurge for the comforts."

The sparkling, blue water of Maple Lake flew past as we drove. Cara could be a little bit of a lead foot behind the wheel, but she was an excellent driver and always in control. I relaxed even more and enjoyed the view of rolling, green hills rimming the lake. The water was dotted with white sails as many people took advantage of this glorious summer day.

Unfortunately, the sails brought my mind back to Hillner's murder. "How on earth am I supposed to find out if any of the suspects sail?"

Cara glanced my way. "Are we back to the murder? I thought you were finally letting go and relaxing over there."

"I was." I pointed out the window. "But the sailboats reminded me."

She turned on her right turn signal to enter the parking lot for the lake's recreational area activities. There was a public boat launch here, restrooms, and the little summer camp every Maple Hills kid attended since time immemorial. There was a small sailing school, where people could also rent the boats to take out on the lake for the day.

The lot was crowded, but Cara managed to squeeze her SUV into a tiny spot. It was a little close to the car next to us, so I opened the door a crack and slithered out, being careful not to ding its door.

"I need to get Charlotte over there." Cara pointed way on the other side of the lot.

"I think I'll just stroll down by the lake and take in the view. I haven't been out here yet, and I forgot how beautiful it is."

She strode across the lot, and I meandered down to the water line by the sailing school and gazed out across the lake. The sun glinted off the water, and I was glad I'd worn my sunglasses.

"Hello, Amanda. Fancy meeting you here."

I turned to see who spoke and saw Pen Adams approach with a wide smile on his face. He work khaki pants, a navy polo shirt, and deck shoes. By his side strolled Magdalena Hillner, dressed in an outfit far too chic for a day at the Lake in rustic Maple Hills. She looked like an exotic flower in a field of wildflowers. Oh, yeah. And she scowled at me, leaving no question in my mind she was less happy to see me than Pen was.

"Hello, Pen. Magdalena. What are you doing here?"

They reached my side and stopped. Pen gestured behind him. "We heard about the sailboat rentals here at the lake, and I thought it would be an excellent way to take both our minds off ... well ... you know." His voice trailed off at the end.

"My husband's brutal murder. Probably at the hands of a jealous lover," Magdalena interjected. She pulled her sunglasses down on her face and peered at me pointedly over their frames.

I chose to ignore the ludicrous insinuation I was her husband's killer. Instead, I turned my gaze to Pen and said, "What a good idea. Nothing soothes the soul so much as a day out on Maple Lake. I've lived in big cities for so long, I'd almost forgotten how peaceful it is here."

"Living in Manhattan, I know exactly what you mean. But I do have my own sailboat, and I get out on the water as often as I can," Pen said with a wistful gaze out over the water.

"Your sailboat is much more luxurious than these." Magdalena chuffed out a breath. "I enjoy our time on it much more than on the dinghy we rented this morning."

"I'm sorry you didn't enjoy it, my dear." Pen rubbed Magdalena's shoulder. "You are always so relaxed on my boat, I thought it would be the perfect thing to help you forget your troubles for an hour."

"Because you own a sailing yacht, Pen. These are barely boats."

One side of Pen's mouth quirked up, and he shrugged. "I just love sailing so much, I don't care if I'm on a sixty-footer or a dinghy."

My eyes widened beneath my sunglasses. It was a

sleuthing gift from the gods. I'd been wondering how to find out if our suspects sailed, and here was Pen volunteering the information he was an expert sailor, while Magdalena didn't seem to have enough knowledge or interest in sailing to know about the ropes and knotmaking. But what motive could the wealthy and powerful theater producer have for murdering the director of his new show? I realized I'd been silent for a few beats too long while I pondered this new information, when Pen cleared his throat and looked at me quizzically.

"I've only ever sailed on these little guys on this lake. But I love it." I paused and then added, "I contacted the theater volunteers this morning about the production going on, and I'll need to head back to the theater later this afternoon to work out a schedule. Will either of you be there?"

"At the site of my beloved Aaron's murder? I think not." Magdalena clutched her chest.

It seemed to me like she was laying it on a bit thick. Aaron was not exactly husband of the year, and their marriage had serious issues. But her talking about the theater reminded me of a question I had for her. Since the widow had made no secret of the fact she suspected me, I decided to return the favor and not sugarcoat it. "I've been meaning to ask you. What were you doing at the theater that morning? The only car there when I arrived was Aaron's. And you were in workout clothes. Did you jog there or something?"

"Jog? Me?" She snorted delicately and waved her hand. "Never. I rode in with Aaron, so I could take a stroll through the woods. The night before, at that ghastly little bar, someone told me there were lovely walking trails there."

"That explains it then," I said.

"Amanda, sorry to interrupt, but we've got to get Charlotte to the Y for her swim practice," Cara's voice called across the parking lot.

I looked her way and waved, and then turned back to Pen and Magdalena. "That's my ride; I've got to run."

He waggled his eyebrows at me, "I was actually thinking of swinging by the library after I drop Magdalena off at the hotel to try to find your lovely aunt. Perhaps convince her to join me for dinner."

"Aunt Lori has a packed social calendar, but it's worth a try. If I don't see you at the theater later, Maple Hills is a small town, I'm sure I'll see you around."

"I'll be waiting with bated breath," Magdalena said.

I trotted back to Cara's SUV and mulled over our conversation. I couldn't get a handle on Pen. He and Magdalena were coproducers on the show, but with their talk of sailing together on Pen's yacht, it seemed like they had a personal friendship in addition to their working relationship. I'd be interested to find out how they met originally. Did their friendship predate her marriage to Aaron? I wasn't picking up on an attraction vibe from Pen toward Magdalena. His interest in her was more fatherly. And I knew if a man treated me as badly as Aaron treated his wife, my father wouldn't take kindly to it. Was Pen angry enough about Aaron's blatant infidelities and disrespect of Magdalena to kill Aaron?

Pen was a sailor with a knowledge of knots and ropes. And to know Aaron was to hate him, so perhaps he had yet another motive for killing him? Something to do with their work together?

Really it could be anything. It would be easier to find one killer with a motive if Aaron had just been less of a jerk. As it stood, people could've been lining up to murder him for a multitude of reasons.

After Cara dropped me off on her way to the Y, I rushed in the house to take care of Fluffy. I hadn't brought her with me to Cara's, because I hadn't realized we'd be eating outside. Cara had an ancient and very cranky cat. Which would have made having lunch inside her house problematic, as Fluffy did not get along with cats. Or other dogs. Or many people besides me. I guess I had to admit, if only to myself, I kinda got why everyone called her The Beast. But with me, she was a sweetheart.

Usually. Based on the glare she bestowed upon me when I opened her crate, and the way she snubbed me as I hustled around the kitchen, loading what we'd need into my designer tote bag, I was still in the doghouse with my girl. Oh well, she'd come around. She always got a little testy when I left her alone for too long.

"Don't worry, Fluff. You're coming to the theater with me. And tonight, it's just you and me, here in the house like buddies. I promise."

She hoisted her plumed tail over her back, and it drifted back and forth. Not exactly an enthusiastic wag, but as predicted, she was coming out of her snit.

By the time we arrived at the Theater in the Pines, all was forgiven, and she trotted by my side on her leash with a bouncing gait.

We entered the lobby, and Jeremy popped out of his office. "Amanda, I'm so glad you're here, I wanted to talk to you about ... y'know... " He paused and the wide grin faded off his face. "You brought The Beast."

"I had no choice. I didn't bring her to Cara's, and then I went with Cara to pick up Charlotte at the lake. Long story short, I was away longer than her majesty liked, and I needed to redeem myself."

"Plus you felt guilty you left her alone and don't want her to be too upset," Jeremy said.

"Also true. You know me too well."

"You're such a sucker for that dog."

He gestured for me to follow him into his office. He shut the door behind us and scooted around to sit behind his desk. My overfilled tote bag landed with a thump when I dropped it on the ground, and I picked up Fluffy to hold in my lap while we talked. Jeremy was right. I was an utter and complete sap where Fluffy was concerned.

"Something interesting happened while I was at the lake. About the case."

"Do tell," Jeremy put his elbows on his desk and leaned forward.

"I ran into Pen Adams and Magdalena Hillner there. They'd been sailing." I made a popping sound, mimed dropping a microphone, and sat back in my chair to await his response.

He gasped, put both hands over his heart and flopped back in his chair. "Here we were wanting to know which of our suspects sailed, and this gets dropped right into your lap."

"I know, right? What are the odds?"

"Slim to none. So, Pen and Magdalena both sail?"

I shook my head. "Only Pen, I think. She was more of a passenger. But, he's sailed his whole life. Even owns his own sailing yacht."

"Good work."

"The one thing I keep wondering is what possible motive Pen could have." I petted the top of Fluffy's head, and took one of her velvety ears between my fingers and rubbed.

"I've been wondering if he had the hots for Aaron's wife," Jeremy said.

"I thought the same thing." With my free hand I swung two fingers between my eyes and his. "You and I have always been so in sync." I paused and screwed up my mouth. "But then he said he was going to drop Magdalena off at the hotel and go to the library to see Aunt Lori and ask her to dinner."

"Which doesn't sound like a man infatuated enough with Magdalena to kill for her." Jeremy heaved a sigh. "Back to the drawing board."

"Do you know if Aaron and Pen had a personal relationship, aside from the business one?" I asked.

He swung his head back and forth. "I do not. But I know they've worked together on previous productions."

"Could there be some reason a producer would want to do away with a director? I mean, Aaron was difficult to get along with, but as the producer, couldn't Pen just fire him?"

"Maybe, maybe not. Depends on the contract they have." Jeremy gazed at the ceiling and tapped his index finger on his lips. "There could be a financial motive."

"Always a strong motive, according to the mysteries I read. What would it be? I mean, Pen is invested, literally, in Aaron's success with this play, right?"

"Yes. But maybe no."

"Could you be more cryptic?" I huffed out a breath, and Fluffy shook her head as it tickled her. "Sorry, girl."

"I know for a big Broadway show, the producers carry all kinds of insurance. Some is liability, say if a performer or audience member is injured. But some is if the production can't go on for some reason, say there's a big-name star who is carrying the show, and they can't perform for an extended period of time for illness or something."

My years of dealing with insurance as the VP of Human Resources kicked in, and my brain shifted into that mode. "I see. So, if Aaron is killed and the show doesn't go on, then as the producer, Pen might collect a sizeable insurance payout."

"Bing, bing, bing. Give the lady a prize."

"Except, Pen decided the show is going on, so the insurance theory doesn't work."

"Hmm, you're right. Let me think."

We sat in silence for a moment, until an idea occurred to me. "Okay, this might be too twisted and devious—"

"We're talking about someone who set up Aaron to get crushed by lighting equipment in the hopes it would look like an accident. I think we can take twisted and devious as a given," Jeremy interrupted me.

"Right. So, what if Pen is just paying lip service to carrying on with the show? He's taking over as director temporarily, maybe he's going to make such a hash of it the show will never make it to Broadway without Hillner as the director. Could he collect then?"

"It depends on the policy, but it's definitely a possible motive." Jeremy's jaw dropped, and he snapped his fingers. "For both the producers. Don't forget, Magdalena is a producer too. She'd profit as well as Pen."

"Interesting. But of course, the person who most wanted the production to not make it to Broadway is Melville Dickens. And he is currently without an alibi. I need to hunt him down and find out where he was."

"And I'd hate to think it's a local, but Kaylee Tufton, her dad, and her boyfriend were all angry enough to have killed him too."

"You're right. But first, I need to get to my office and set up the volunteer schedule. Keep your fingers crossed we have enough kids still willing to work, because if not ... you, Cara, and I will be recreating our youth as ushers here." I stood up and placed Fluffy on the floor. As I slung my tote bag over my shoulder, a thought struck me. "And even more important, I need to call Aunt Lori to warn her about Pen Adams. If he's the killer, going out on a date with him could be fatal."

Chapter Ten

I had stayed up way too late working on my book, but my job at the theater, reconnecting with my friends, and sleuthing were taking up too much of my time during the day. I smothered a yawn as I held the hose on my mother's flowerbed in front of the house. Fluffy flopped on the ground nearby, basking in the warmth of the sun, with her leash looped around a wrought iron post designed for just that purpose. My dad bought it; since Fluffy was a city dog, he worried she might take off from the yard, but wanted us to be able to enjoy the outdoors too. Her eyes closed in bliss, she exhaled with a grunt, and it was safe to say Fluffy was enjoying her time in the yard.

A few minutes later, she suddenly lifted her head, stared in the direction of Cara's parents' house next door, and growled low in her throat. I looked over and saw Cara's dad walking towards us.

"Welcome home, Amanda! Sorry I haven't been over to see you yet."

"Hi, Mr. Rosenberg. No worries, I'm sorry too. I've

been meaning to stop by to see you and Mrs. R., but I've been so busy since I got here."

He enveloped me in a bear bug, which was appropriate, because he was a burly, giant of a man. Mrs. Rosenberg was as tiny as he was big, and Cara took after her mom. Fluffy jumped up and barked, but when she realized he wasn't a threat to me, she plopped back down on the ground and resumed her sunbath.

He stepped back and beamed at me. "Cara has been so excited about living in the same town as you again."

"Me too. I missed her and Jeremy when I was in LA."

"I have to confess something to you, kiddo." He rubbed the back of his neck.

"What?" I couldn't imagine what sort of deep, dark confession Mr. Rosenberg would have to make. He was one of the kindest men I've ever known.

"I didn't come over here just to say 'hi'. I wanted to ask you a favor."

"Anything."

His smile was brighter than the sun. "You are such a good girl. Your parents must be so proud of you. No hesitation. No questions. Just willing to help. What if I was asking you to rob a bank or something?"

I burst out laughing. "I can't imagine a bank heist is the favor you need."

"It's not," he admitted with a sheepish grin. "I just need a lift to the post office. My car is in the shop, and I need to get a package shipped out today."

"Which is way better than being an accomplice to a felony. Sure thing. Just let me run inside, clean up a little, and get my stuff. Meet you in the driveway in fifteen minutes?"

"Perfect. Thanks so much, Amanda."

Fluffy and I sat on a bench in front of the brick post office on Main Street, while Mr. Rosenberg ran inside to mail his box. We were in the shade of the building, so it was a cool, comfortable place to people watch.

A few minutes later, Cara's dad emerged from the post office with another man. He looked to be in his forties, with a craggy face and a weary expression. I didn't recognize him, but he fell into an age range that was older than me, but younger than my parents, so I could see how I wouldn't know him.

I put Fluffy down on the sidewalk and stood up to greet them.

"Amanda, this is Larry Tufton. Larry, this is Amanda Seldon. She's Michael and Becky's daughter, back from the wilds of Los Angeles."

The man's face reddened, and he glared at me. "Amanda Seldon? From the Theater in the Pines?"

I recognized his name as Kaylee Tufton's father, but I couldn't imagine why he would be so angry with me.

"Yes. I'm the volunteer coordinator there this summer."

"Pfft. And what did you do in your role as volunteer coordinator—" he made air quotes around the last two words "—to protect my daughter from predators while she was volunteering at your theater?"

Mr. Rosenberg held up his hands. "Hey now, Larry. Calm down."

I flashed my friend's father a quick grin. "It's okay. The original volunteer coordinator had to step down, and I just began the job a couple of days ago. I've only met your daughter briefly."

He sputtered, as if my comment had deflated his anger

a bit, but his fists were still clenched by his side. "She's an innocent child, and someone should've been protecting her from scum like Aaron Hillner."

While Kaylee was younger than Hillner, and I didn't know about her level of innocence before she met Hillner, she was above the age of consent. And short of throwing myself between them at the Hitchcock Tavern, like a Victorian chaperone, I don't know what I could've done to keep them apart. But he was her dad, and I understood his emotions too. I was thirty-five and my dad still called me his 'baby girl'.

Luckily, Mr. Rosenberg's peacekeeping skills came into play. "We can't protect our kids forever, Larry, much as we'd like to. Kaylee is in her twenties now and has to make her own decisions. Even if they're not great ones, hopefully, she'll learn from them and do better next time."

The decision to have an affair with the married Hillner most certainly qualified as 'not great', but if she'd killed him in a fit of jealous rage that would be a whole other level of bad decision making.

"Hillner took advantage of my daughter. And I'm glad he's dead. Good riddance."

And on that cheery note, Tufton turned on his heel and stormed down the sidewalk.

"Larry's always had blinders about Kaylee and a short fuse on his temper." Mr. Rosenberg shook his head and tsked his tongue.

I watched Larry Tufton stomp down the street and shoulder a woman pushing a stroller out of his way. The man was a tinder keg, ready to blow. Had finding his daughter in a compromising position with Aaron Hillner caused his short fuse to ignite into fury? And was he furious enough to have killed him?

I LEANED MY HEAD THROUGH THE FRONT DOOR OF THE library and breathed a sigh of relief at the sight of Aunt Lori straight ahead of me at the circulation desk. "I have Fluffy with me, is it okay if we come in?"

"Of course. Good to see you, Mandy-bel."

"Thanks. I'll hold her the whole time." I shifted my tote bag, which had slipped, back up over my shoulder and strolled to the desk.

Aunt Lori leaned down and sat back up with a pile of dusty, old tomes in her hand. "Here are the books you wanted for your research. After we talked yesterday, I pulled them all and checked them out to you."

"Great, thanks." I wrinkled my nose and looked at my already full tote bag. I'd have to squeeze them in somehow.

"You can put The Beast down while you put them away. There are only one or two people here this morning."

I bent over to put Fluffy on the floor, but kept a tight grip on the leash. As I stowed the books in the bag, I asked, "How was your date with Pen? Thanks for texting me when you got home, by the way. I was worried about you."

"You always were a worrier. It was a very enjoyable evening. He's a good bit older than me, but so sophisticated and debonair." The corners of her mouth tilted up in a devilish grin. "Plus I got to play amateur sleuth. See if I could find out anything to link him to Hillner's murder."

I hoisted my tote bag onto the counter, where it landed with a resounding thump. I was going to pick Fluffy back up, but she sat peacefully at my feet, so I decided to let her be. Plus it gave my arms a rest. Lugging her and my tote bag around all the time was tiring, but maybe I'd end up with cut biceps from it.

"And did you?" I asked.

She waggled her hands. "Not really. He kept trying to talk about other things. Like how beautiful I am, which I have to admit is a tempting thing to let him keep saying." She chuckled. "But I did my best to bring the conversation back to Hillner and his murder. I confirmed what you learned at the lake. He's an accomplished sailor, and knows a lot about ropes and the old hemp house theater setup, so he had the knowledge to bring the light down."

"But like you said, he's no spring chicken. Could he have done it physically? Gotten up into the rafters?"

Aunt Lori rolled her eyes. "Trust me, Pen is spry. We danced a little, and he was very muscular under those old money, preppy clothes he wears. And he had a lot of stamina on the dance floor. More than me, I have to admit. I was ready to sit down and have a cocktail long before he was."

"Then the question isn't could he have committed the crime, but did he? What did your gut tell you last night?"

"I enjoyed my evening, and I don't want to think Pen killed Hillner, but I honestly don't know if you can rule him out of your investigation just yet."

The tag's on Fluffy's collar jingled, and I glanced down at her. She stood and wagged, with a happy expression on her doggie face. I followed the direction of her gaze, and a happy expression spread across my human face too. It was Dylan.

He emerged from the stacks carrying a couple of hardback books. But he wasn't smiling back at me. When he spoke, it was a combination of exasperation and worry. "*Your* investigation, Amanda? Don't tell me you're still looking into the play director's death. It's a dangerous hobby, and my brother is a pro."

My lips formed a straight line, and I narrowed my eyes

at him. "And is your brother, the pro, still considering me a suspect?"

Dylan handed his books to Aunt Lori. She clicked away on her computer keyboard, and the scanner beeped as it read the barcodes on the books.

He scuffed his toes on the carpeted floor. "Maybe. But he will find the killer, I promise."

"Until he does, I can't promise I won't keep looking for myself."

"I guess I understand." He took the books Aunt Lori handed him, and flashed a smile at me. "Are we still friends?"

"Of course we are, as long as *you* don't think I'm a murderer, like your brother does."

DYLAN AND I EXITED THE LIBRARY TOGETHER. FLUFFY pranced between us on the sidewalk, and gazed adoringly up at him. I couldn't blame her. If it was socially acceptable for me to do so, I would be prancing and gazing at him too.

"Where are you headed?" Dylan asked.

"I'm parked in the municipal lot by the Green. I need to get over to the theater."

"Me too. Well, I'm parked in the municipal lot. I don't need to go to the theater."

I held back a smile at his cute clarification. "I understood."

His face brightened. "I get a little flustered around you."

"Around me?" My eyes widened, and my jaw dropped, and I could hear my late grandmother's voice in my head asking if I was trying to catch flies. I snapped it shut.

"Sure." He glanced away and bobbed his head. "Confession time, Amanda. I had a huge crush on you in high school."

Grandma Seldon would be so disappointed in me, because my jaw once again hung open somewhere in the vicinity of the sidewalk. My heart raced. "No way."

"Way."

"But you were—" I waved my hand from his head to his toes and back up again. "—you. You were so popular. And I so wasn't."

He shrugged. "The whole high school popularity thing is weird. Since I swam and played baseball, I got lumped in with the so-called popular crowd. But I didn't have a lot in common with most of them. And everyone was so busy trying to maintain their images, no one got to know each other in any real way. You always had such a deep friendship with Cara and Jeremy, I was a little jealous."

"You were jealous of three dorks like us?" I narrowed my eyes at him. He seemed sincere, but I couldn't help but be gobsmacked by his revelation.

"Sure. You were so tight. And you always had each other's backs. And you were all just who you were, and accepted each other unconditionally. I used to imagine if we dated, I could be the Fourth Musketeer." He lowered his gaze and his cheeks flamed red.

"But you never asked me out."

"No. I was too shy around girls back then, and I was too afraid of getting shot down."

"Wow. Just ... wow." Dylan's confession tilted my world on its axis, and I couldn't get anything more coherent or profound out of my mouth.

"And suddenly, I'm afraid of getting shot down again."

I reached out and grasped his bicep, which I discovered was firm and strong. "No. I'm just speechless. I would definitely not have shot you down in high school, and I won't now either. Although in high school, I might've thought you were asking me out as some kind of cruel prank, like in that horror novel." I winked at him.

"I would never," he said.

"I know. Now. But I was more insecure in high school." I glanced down at Fluffy and then peeked up at Dylan through my lashes. "And if we're both going to be honest, I had a pretty big crush on you back then too."

"No way," he repeated my earlier words to him. And Grandma Seldon would also have something to say about his slack jaw as he stared at me.

"Way."

"What do we do now? Do you have the time to grab a cup of coffee before you get to the theater?"

I really didn't, but there was no way I was going to say no to Dylan Carlow after he admitted his high school crush. "Maybe a quick one."

"Great." He smiled at me, and took my hand as we strolled toward the Sit and Sip.

His hand was big, warm, and a little bit rough from working in the orchard. It was every high school dream I had of holding hands with him while walking down the halls of Hills Regional High come true.

"Isn't this a picture? My brother holding hands with a suspect in my murder investigation."

Fantasy ended, and back to the real world. The one where Dylan's brother was the chief of police and believed I was capable of killing Aaron Hillner. Not the most auspicious start to a new relationship.

Chapter Eleven

Fluffy growled once and then barked as she charged toward the police chief.

Dylan bent down and shushed her in a soothing manner. "Shh ... don't worry, little girl. He's my brother."

His words and calm tone of voice did the trick, and she stopped barking and allowed him to pick her up and hold her. Which was an amazing enough feat I might have to start dating him just to keep him around for Fluffy wrangling when she went into beast mode.

"Don't you two look cozy," the chief observed with a frown.

"Back off, Danny." Dylan scowled at his brother.

The chief held up his hands. "Just making an observation. No need to get all hot under the collar.

"I notice you still called me a suspect, chief. Haven't you been able to confirm through my friends in LA that I wasn't carrying on a secret affair with Aaron Hillner?"

He heaved a sigh. "If you're going to be walking down the street holding hands with my little brother, you might as well call me Danny."

His words made a tightness in my chest I hadn't even noticed before ease. "Okay, Danny. Call me Amanda. Your favorite suspect."

"Not my favorite, just one I can't take off the table yet. See the thing is, it's harder to prove you know someone than to prove you don't. None of your friends or coworkers have reported you knew him, but if it was a clandestine affair with a married man, they wouldn't realize he existed."

"And until you do..." My voice trailed off at the end with a sigh of defeat.

"Until I do, you're still on my white board at the office."

"There are plenty of other suspects." I paused and looked around, only to find a sidewalk full of people casting openly curious glances our way. I stepped closer to Danny and lowered my voice. "For example, did you know Pen Adams is an accomplished sailor, and very physically fit, so he could've manipulated the rope to make the light fall. Plus, as the producer, he might have a financial incentive for Aaron to be dead, through production insurance."

Danny pressed his lips together, but the twinkle in his eyes told me he was one second away from bursting out in laughter. "He's very physically fit, huh? Might I ask how you know that factoid, Nancy Drew?"

Dylan chuckled next to me.

I narrowed my eyes to glare at him. "Traitor."

Dylan fought a losing battle against a grin and said, "I'd kind of like to know how you know about the old guy's physical abilities myself."

"Not how both of you think, obviously. My Aunt Lori went on a date with him last night and informed me he could tear up the dance floor."

Then all three of us burst into laughter.

Danny swiped at his eyes as he caught his breath. "You might just be good enough for my brother after all, Amanda Seldon."

"Good enough to wipe her off your whiteboard?" Dylan asked.

The smile faded from Danny's face. "Not yet."

Oh, well. It looked like I was still on the case to clear my name.

"Sorry we ran out of time to get that coffee together," Dylan said as we walked toward the parking lot.

"It's okay. It was a good chance to try to clear the air with your brother."

Dylan grimaced. "About that, sorry you're still a suspect."

I raised one shoulder in a shrug. "I understand why he can't let me off the hook yet, but it makes me all the more determined to clear my name."

"I get it, even if it makes me worry for you a little bit."

"I'll be cautious. I've never been a reckless person. You heard my Aunt Lori back at the library, I presume. I've always been a worrier. And the way I deal with it is by trying to solve whatever is concerning me. Right now, I'm worried I'm going to spend the rest of my days wearing a hideous prison jumpsuit for a crime I didn't commit. I mean, who'd take care of Fluffy? You seem to be the only person besides me she can stand here in Maple Hills."

We'd reached my car by then, and I fumbled in the tote bag that ate Maple Hills for my car keys. I pulled them out of its near bottomless depths and unlocked my car with a click and a beep of the fob.

Dylan handed Fluffy to me. Let me clarify, he handed a

decidedly reluctant-to-be-released-Fluffy to me. She twisted her head to cast a longing glance his way. Did she even bat her long, doggie eyelashes? What a little vixen.

"I see what you mean." Dylan reached out to pat her head between her ears. "And if you get sent to the big house, I'll take care of Fluffy. But you won't be. Like I told you before, Danny is a good cop above all else. He'll find the real killer. Or you will, since you're so determined. Either way, you're in the clear, right?"

"Right." I nodded my head once sharply. I secured Fluffy in the back seat, but didn't shut the door yet, as I wanted to say goodbye to Dylan, because if I did, her early abandonment issues would make her bark to raise the dead. Which might not be a bad thing, if the dead person she raised was Aaron Hillner, then he could tell us exactly what happened to him.

"How about tomorrow?" Dylan asked.

"Tomorrow?"

"For coffee. Since we couldn't have it today, I was hoping maybe we could meet tomorrow morning at the same time at the Sit and Sip. Maybe talk over what's happening here." He gestured between us.

"I'd like that. Ten o'clock?"

His face lit up. "Ten at the Sit and Sip. See you then."

He leaned down and pressed a light kiss to my cheek. My heart fluttered.

But before we could speak, I heard the voice of another angry man behind me and turned to see who it was. First Larry Tufton, then Chief Carlow, and now Caleb Symansky. All lining up to yell at me. How delightful.

"You're the lady in charge of the volunteers at the theater, aren't you? I've got a bone to pick with you."

I took a deep breath before I spoke. "You're Caleb, right? Kaylee's boyfriend?"

"Kaylee's *ex*-boyfriend." He crossed his arms and glowered at me, but I noticed the hint of moisture in his eyes.

"I'm sorry. I can see you're hurt," I said.

"Me too, Caleb. But it's not Ms. Seldon's fault," Dylan added.

"I thought with that Hillner dude dead, this play would be cancelled, and everything would go back to normal. But now the show is going on, and Kaylee is fighting with her parents about still volunteering at the theater as a way to freaking honor that jerk Hillner."

"None of it was my decision, Caleb." I held up my hands palms up, while Fluffy began to bark from the car.

Dylan leaned into to soothe her again. Seriously, the man was like the Fluffy Whisperer.

"I guess, but you emailed her about coming back to work. Her dad told me."

"I emailed all the volunteers about coming back. Since the producers decided to continue with the production of *Ecstasy in the Aspens*, as the volunteer coordinator, I need to get a schedule together and get everyone trained on their tasks. I did not email Kaylee specifically."

With Fluffy calm again, Dylan straightened up and grasped Caleb's shoulder. "What's really bothering you, man? I know you're not truly angry at Ms. Seldon, are you?"

A tear fell from Caleb's eye, and he wiped it away. "I guess not. I just thought with Hillner out of the picture, Kaylee would come back to me, and everything would go back to normal with us. But it hasn't happened. She's still crazy about him, and now that he's dead, she'll never see his true colors. He'll always be this big, romantic fantasy for her. And I can't compete with a fantasy."

It was a surprisingly insightful observation from Caleb, who hadn't struck me as one of life's deep thinkers before. My heart caught a little for him. I could tell he was heartbroken, and what's more ... he was right.

"I know what you mean. Kaylee didn't really love Hillner. She loved a fantasy of him. Because, let me tell you, the real Aaron Hillner was a class-A jerk. She's still besotted now, but hopefully, she'll come around to see the truth."

"And if she doesn't?" Caleb snuffled. "What good is Hillner being dead, if she doesn't realize she really loves me?"

Dylan and I exchanged a quick glance, and his wide eyes mirrored my own.

"What are you saying, Caleb?" Dylan asked.

"Nothing. Just forget I said anything." The young man's sneakers squeaked on the pavement as he broke into a run and took off across the parking lot.

I blinked once. Twice. And swung my head around to look at Dylan. "Did he just say what I think he said?"

"I'm not sure. He definitely wanted Hillner out of the way, so he could get back with Kaylee."

"But did he want him out of the way enough to kill him?"

By the time I reached the theater and got Fluffy settled in my office, I still pondered the likelihood of Caleb as the killer.

I smothered a yawn and regretted the fact we didn't have a chance to get a coffee downtown. There was a coffee maker backstage, and I decided to get a cup, a big cup, before I started work.

Leaving Fluffy ensconced on her dog bed in my office, I shut the door behind me and cut through the theater to get backstage. As I climbed the steps to the stage, I shuddered when I recalled the last time I'd done this. I scurried past the spot where Aaron's body had lain as quickly as possible.

When I reached the coffee maker, I selected the biggest mug I could find, popped a full-caf pod into the machine, and pressed the start button. The machine began to hum, and I looked around me.

There was a rehearsal scheduled this afternoon, so it was too early for any cast members to be here, although a few crew members were busy at work. The machine beeped, I grabbed my mug, and my eyelids fluttered shut as I inhaled the heavenly aroma.

"You're related to the librarian, right?"

A man's voice spoke behind me, and I jumped. A little hot coffee sloshed on my hand, and I'm not too proud to say I licked it off, rather than waste a drop of precious caffeine. I turned to see who spoke and saw Melville Dickens, in his usual state of disarray.

He had dark circles under his eyes, and his clothes looked like they could use a run through a washing machine. I wondered if there was a way to subtly direct him to the laundromat in town.

"I am. Amanda Seldon. I'm also the volunteer coordinator here at the theater. We've met before." A couple of times, I added silently. The man was so self-absorbed, he wasn't capable of remembering anything not directly related to his perceived literary genius.

"Right, right. I was pleased to know my original work was so popular here in Maple Hills. At least a lot of people here will have read *Agony in the Aspens* the way I intended the story to be told, and not just see this travesty of a production."

Honestly, the man only knew one song, and he sang it until he lost his voice. We get it, we get it, you hate this play. Sheesh, did he never talk about anything else?

"What are you working on now?" I asked, in the hope of getting him on another topic.

"Nothing. My despair over this farcical play has dried up my creative juices. I can't write a word." He raked his hands through his hair, and it stood out at even wilder angles than before. Like Einstein with dark hair.

"What a shame. Perhaps you should distance yourself from the production, for your own peace of mind."

He narrowed his eyes and looked all around us. "I want to keep an eye on things here. Especially with Hillner dead, perhaps there's a chance I can influence Pen into creating a production more in line with my vision."

Hmm, Melville hoped to benefit from Hillner's death. Enough to kill him?

Which reminded me. "I have a question for you."

"You do? Is it about writing? Your aunt told me you were an aspiring novelist."

"Um, no, not right now. Perhaps another time. I wanted to ask you something else. You see, I ran into Mrs. Godfrey recently."

"Mrs. Godfrey?" He furrowed his brow and squinted. "Who's she?"

"She owns the Dew Drop Inn, where you told me you were staying. She suffers from insomnia and noticed your car wasn't at the hotel the night or the morning of Hillner's death. I wondered where you might have been? Maple Hills isn't exactly an open-all-hours kind of town, so there was no place for you to go at that hour."

"Why do you want to know where I was?" He bounced on his feet. "Are you some sort of super fan?"

Not even my desire for information to solve Hillner's murder and clear my name would allow me to let this man think I was a super fan. "No. Actually, I'm sorry to say I've never read *Agony in the Aspens*."

His face fell. "Oh. I see. You really should, especially as an aspiring writer. It would be like a masterclass in creating fiction for you. So, why do you want to know where I was?"

I wish I could say I thought quickly on my feet and came up with a clever cover story, but I didn't. I froze, and being a terrible liar, I blurted out, "Because I'm trying to find out who killed Aaron Hillner."

"Why? What does it matter to you?"

"It's self-preservation. The chief of police is investigating me as a possible suspect, and I'd like to find the real killer before I get arrested for a crime I didn't commit."

His eyes bugged. "And you think I'm the real killer? You're trying to find out where I was around the time he was murdered."

"I don't mean to be insulting—"

"Then you're failing miserably, because I can't think of anything more insulting than calling a man a murderer. Which, I am not, by the way."

"Then you won't mind telling me where you were."

He screwed up his mouth and stared at me for several beats. Finally he spoke, "Fine. I'll tell you. I was surrounding myself with nature, in the hopes of it stirring my muse."

"Okay, I don't know what that means."

"It means I drove my car to the lake, where I parked and then walked on the trails in the woods. I'd hoped being closer to the wonders of nature would help defeat this writer's block."

"Did it help?"

"No." He shook his head mournfully. "It did not. The water is really what soothes my soul, so I had rented a sail-boat for the week. One of those little ones at the rental place at the lake. I didn't want to go out alone on the lake at night, so I wandered around until dawn, and as soon as I saw the rosy fingers of Aurora in the sky, I took to the water."

"Very poetic," I said.

"Thank you. My work has been highly praised by critics for its classical allusions and poetic beauty."

"Which is very nice for you, but unfortunately, it's not a very good alibi." I took a deep sip of my coffee.

"What do you mean?'

"You were alone in the woods and on the lake during the time Hillner was probably killed. No one can vouch for your whereabouts. When you came back in on the sailboat, was the rental place open yet?"

"No. It was still very early. The water failed to stir my creative juices the way it usually does. Perhaps because it's a lake and not the ocean. I normally sail on the ocean. The waves are so raw and powerful, like my words."

"You're a frequent sailor, then?" I asked.

"Yes. I have a little place on the shore in Connecticut, and I sail every chance I can."

Melville Dickens had just jumped up on my suspect list. He had motive, no alibi, and as an experienced sailor, he knew his way around ropes.

Chapter Twelve

I shut down my laptop and closed the lid with a snap. Finally. I'd finished the volunteer schedule and could dive into the library books Aunt Lori loaned me. I fought the urge to rub my hands together like a cartoon villain. Would a normal person be this excited about doing research? I didn't think so, but I was okay with it.

"Are you still here, Amanda?" Jeremy's voice called from the lobby.

"Yep, in my office," I called back to him.

He poked his head around the partially open door. "What are you doing?"

"I just finished the schedule. It took longer than I antic-ipated. There were some issues with people not responding to my email, so then I had to text and call them. Annoying. But it's done now."

"Did we end up with enough volunteers to staff the place?"

"We did." I nodded once. "Only a couple of kids dropped out, but most will still be here. Including Kaylee, which does not please her boyfriend at all. I ran into him earlier. With Hillner gone, he thought Kaylee would come running back to him."

"Seriously? And he's admitting it to people, even though the man was murdered? Doesn't he realize it makes him look suspicious?"

"He was very emotional. I don't think he's thinking clearly. What I don't know is if it's because he's twenty or because he just murdered a man to get his ex-girlfriend back and is frustrated the plan didn't work."

"Don't stay too late, okay? You're the last one here. Do you remember how to set the alarm when you leave?"

"I do. You've shown me how to do it more than once. I'll be fine."

"There was a murder here a few days ago, so I think it's reasonable to worry about you being alone here."

I jerked my head toward the dog bed, where Fluffy had just awoken. Her whiskers were smooshed up one side of her face, and she blinked owlishly. Until she saw Jeremy and then she growled. "I'm not alone. I have my guard shih tzu with me."

Jeremy took a step backward. "She's enough to frighten even the most hardened killer."

My phone buzzed on the desk, and I glanced down to see a video call notification. "Oh! It's my mom." I held the phone up in front of my face and tapped the screen to answer. "Hi, Mommy."

"Hello, darling," she answered.

"Hiya, Mama Seldon." Jeremy skirted around the desk, carefully on the side Fluffy wasn't, and waved at the phone. His face split by a wide grin, he waved at my mom with both hands.

And for a second, I saw him as eight-year-old Jeremy waving at my mom when she'd come to pick us up at school. There was something truly special about the friends you've had forever.

"Jeremy, how lovely." My mom clapped her hands and beamed. "Two of the Three Musketeers."

I squinted at the screen. "Where are you guys? Is that the Grand Canyon behind you?"

"It most certainly is. And it is splendid. We are having the time of our lives on this trip. But I hear there's been a murder at the Theater in the Pines, sweetie. Are you okay?"

"There was, but I'm fine."

Jeremy stuck his head in front of mine. "She's more than fine. Ask her about Dylan Carlow. In the meantime, I've got to run, ladies. Eric and I are going out to dinner tonight. Bye." He waved at the screen, pecked me on the cheek, and trotted out the door.

"What about Dylan Carlow? Sunny texted me you two had dinner together at the diner the other night. Are you a thing now?"

"A thing, Mommy?"

"You know, a thing. Are you dating?"

"Maybe. I don't know. We're hanging out a bit. He's a nice guy."

"He's the best. And you've been half in love with him since you were eleven."

"How did you know?" My jaw dropped. I never mentioned my crush to my mom. Seriously, the CIA had nothing on Becky Seldon.

"You used to practice writing Amanda Seldon-Carlow on every piece of scrap paper in the house. It really wasn't too hard to figure out." My mom chuckled. "It was sweet."

I pressed a hand to my heated cheek. "And you will keep that piece of information between us, please. I don't want Dylan to realize what a goober I was. At least not yet. I don't want to scare him off before things even get going."

My mom threw back her head and laughed. "You are such a riot."

"I'm not kidding, Mother."

Which only made her laugh even harder. "I've got to run, sweetie. We're taking a tour, and if I don't rush I'll be late meeting your father. I just wanted to check in to make sure you're okay after the murder in the theater. Stay safe. I love you."

"I love you too, Mommy. I'll talk to you soon."

"Definitely. If I can get a decent Wi-Fi signal, I'll call from the road tomorrow. That way I'll have plenty of time to ask you all about this murder, and the Dylan situation." Another laugh bubbled out of her. "Bye Bye, Mrs. Seldon-Carlow!"

"Mother. Stop," I spoke firmly, but it was to a blank screen, as my mother had already ended our video call.

I dropped into my desk chair, and looked at Fluffy. "Sometimes living anonymously in the big city was easier, wasn't it?"

I RELUCTANTLY CLOSED THE BOOK I WAS READING AND glanced at the time on my phone. Since my office seriously must've been a closet in another life, there was no outside window. As absorbed in my research as I'd been, I hadn't realized how much time had elapsed.

Fluffy must really have to go outside. I glanced her way, and saw her sprawled on the dog bed, snoring gently. I decided to let sleeping dogs lie, and go to the bathroom myself first. I pushed my chair back as slowly as I could, so as not to wake Fluffy, and tiptoed out of the room. I left my office door open behind me, since we were alone in the building.

There were only the dimmest lights on in both the lobby and theater. I shivered. There was definitely a creepier vibe when the building was dark and empty. I hadn't intended to still be here after the sun went down.

I hustled to the ladies' room, and relished the bright, fluorescent lighting. When I was done with my business, I ventured back into the dark lobby, which seemed even darker now my eyes were used to the bright rest room lighting.

When I was halfway across the lobby to my office, a thump sounded from the theater. I froze in my place. Well most of my body froze in place. Except my heart, which pounded out a staccato rhythm. "Hello? Is someone here?" my voice quavered.

Silence. Maybe I'd just imagined the thump. Or maybe Fluffy had woken up and wandered out of the office. I held my hands on my chest over my heart and willed it to slow down. I took several deep breaths, and my body relaxed. I must've just imagined the sound.

Time to get Fluffy, my books, and head for home.

I hadn't taken five steps before another muffled thump sounded from the theater. That was it, we were going home. Now. I took off at a run for my office. Once there, I tapped out a quick text to Jeremy.

—Leaving the theater now. Lost track of time. BTW, I heard something a little while ago. Is anyone supposed to be here tonight??—

Fluffy lifted her head off the dog bed as I rushed in and shoved my books and laptop into my tote bag in a haphazard fashion. I clipped the leash to her collar and said, "C'mon, girl, we're outta here."

At the doorway, I paused long enough to flick the light switch to the off position, and then shut the door behind us. I stopped and listened and heard nothing, and breathed a sigh of relief. It must have just been my imagination, which had always been on the overactive side, according to my parents. It's one of the reasons I loved writing fiction so much, but right now it seemed like more of a negative than a positive.

I stopped walking and my head lolled back on my neck. Darn it all to heck, I still needed to set the alarm system. And it was located by the stage door in the back of the theater. Where my overactive imagination thought it heard thumping.

Oh, well, there was nothing to be done. I had to set the alarm. It was the last thing Jeremy said to me. Plus, I had to have imagined the noises. Or perhaps I really heard something, but misinterpreted what it was. Maybe a squirrel or a raccoon had gotten into the theater and were clomping around. I heaved a sigh. That had to be it. We were in the middle of the woods, after all, it wasn't unheard of for critters to get into the building.

I hustled Fluffy into the theater and rushed down the aisle toward the stage. The dim emergency lighting, which was left on all the time when the theater was in operation, was the only illumination. Once we reached the stage, Fluffy trotted up the steps before me, and I followed along.

On the stage, my dog made a beeline for the very spot I wanted to avoid. The one where we had found Aaron's body. Who knew Fluffy was such a little ghoul?

"Not that way, Fluff. We need to get to the stage door on the other side of the stage." I tugged gently on her leash, but she continued to sniff the wooden floorboards.

While I debated how I could juggle everything else I carried to try to pick her up like a furry football and make a break for the stage door, she finally stopped sniffing and lifted her head.

"That's a good girl, Fluff, let's go home." I turned and walked toward the other side of the stage, but stopped short when the leash pulled taut and wouldn't let me go any further.

I looked back at my dog, only to find her staring fixedly up into the rafters over my head. She growled low in her throat. My gaze nervously flicked in the direction she was peering, and I caught a glimpse of a shadow up above.

Someone was in the rafters.

MY HEART POUNDED SO HARD AGAINST MY RIBCAGE, I feared it was about to break through and flop onto the stage. I tugged hard on the leash, and Fluffy rushed to my side, still staring up and growling. She wasn't barking yet though, which I took as a good sign. Maybe it was just a raccoon or something after all.

Fluffy started barking.

Or maybe it wasn't a raccoon, after all.

"That's it. I'm calling the police." I twisted around to reach my phone in the back pocket of my shorts with my free hand.

The barking stopped abruptly, and I heard a faint whooshing sound come from above me. Fluffy sprinted across the stage. Caught off guard by her sudden movement, she tugged me along behind her. She didn't stop until we reached the wings on the opposite side of the stage.

"Fluff, why couldn't you have run the other way? That's where the stage door and the alarm are."

My answer came in the form of a loud crash on the stage. I looked over my shoulder and saw a piece of lighting equipment, much like the one that had killed

Aaron Hillner. It had plummeted from the rafters down on to the very spot where I'd been standing.

"That's it. Forget the alarm, we are out of here." I flew down the steps and up the aisle for the lobby as if I were in training for the one-hundred meter track and field event at the Olympics.

Behind me, I heard the stage door slam and a squealing of tires from the back parking lot.

At least, it sounded like my attacker had fled the scene. Who could it have been? The back parking lot didn't have its own separate exit. Whoever it was would have to drive around the building to the one and only road out. Maybe if I rushed I could get a glimpse of their car.

I raced through the lobby doors and exited the building, but it was pitch-black outside, and I only caught the merest glimpse of red taillights as the vehicle wended its way down the winding road away from the theater.

My breathing came in harsh pants. I really did need to make time to work out more; I was seriously out of shape if the run from the stage to the front of the theater had me so out of breath.

Or maybe I was just terrified. After all, someone just tried to kill me the way they'd killed Aaron Hillner.

Chapter Thirteen

I locked myself in the car with the engine running, in case a quick getaway became necessary. I called nine-one-one and then Jeremy before I picked up Fluffy from the passenger seat and hugged her to my chest. She nestled the top of her velvety head under my chin, which was her way of hugging me when she was being especially affectionate.

"You saved my life in there, Fluff. Thank you." I pressed a kiss to the top of her head.

Sirens wailed in the distance, and I saw red lights flashing through the woods. I exhaled a breath I'd been unconsciously holding. "Help is on the way, sweet girl."

The police car sped into the lot and parked next to me, with two civilian cars in hot pursuit. When I saw Danny Carlow emerge from the police vehicle, I turned off my car and stepped out of it, still clutching Fluffy.

"You okay, Amanda?" he asked in a manner way more concerned than I would've expected from a man who suspected me of murder.

"I am. Thanks to Fluffy. She let me know something was happening in the rafters and got me out of the way."

"Good dog," Danny reached out to pat her, and Fluffy bared her teeth at him. He pulled his hand back in a sharp motion.

"Sorry about that." I shrugged with a sheepish smile tilting up the corners of my mouth. Fluffy gonna Fluff, what can I say.

Jeremy jumped out of one of the two cars and gravel crunched underfoot as he raced to my side. He held out his arms to hug me, and then noticed Fluffy with her fangs on full display. He stopped in his tracks and retreated a few steps. "I got here as fast as I could. I'm sorry I missed your message. I turned my phone off while we were at the restaurant."

To my surprise, Dylan hopped out of the shiny white pickup truck, which had pulled in right behind the chief. I noticed it had a bright red apple painted on the door with the words, 'Maple Hills Orchards' surrounding it.

He rushed to my side, and Fluffy picked up her head at the sight of him. Her tail brushed my arm as it wagged. He pulled both of us in for a hug, and I caught a peek of Jeremy's incredulous face over Dylan's shoulder.

"How is The Beast allowing him near you?" he asked.

I chuckled, and it quickly turned into borderline hysterical laughter. "She likes Dylan."

He released his hold on me but kept an arm around my shoulders. "I was having dinner with Danny and his family when he got the call. I followed him over here. I hope you don't mind."

"Of course not. The more people here not trying to kill me the better, in my opinion."

"Speaking of trying to kill you. Take me through what happened here tonight," Danny said.

I told him the events of the night, step-by-step.

"And you couldn't tell who it was?" he asked when I was done.

"Nope." I shook my head and put Fluffy on the ground. She might only weigh twelve pounds, but my arms ached from holding her. "I couldn't see anything but taillights in the distance by the time I got out here."

"Car, truck, SUV?" Danny shot the words out like bullets.

"I'm sorry. I couldn't tell. I think maybe car. They might not have been up high enough to be a pickup or a larger SUV. But I just don't know."

"Man or woman?" Danny continued his rapid fire questions.

"It was just a dark shadow. I couldn't tell."

"Let's go inside, and you can show me where it happened." The chief didn't wait for a response, just walked into the theater through the door I'd left open behind me.

I bent down to pick up Fluffy's leash, which released Dylan's arm from around my shoulders. I missed the contact immediately. I was a little chilly, and my always logical brain concluded I had a minor case of shock.

Fluffy led the way into the lobby with me following. Jeremy and Dylan flanked me like bodyguards. We'd just gotten to the stage where Danny stood and stared at the light on the floor and the rope dangling from the rafters above it.

"It's like déjà vu, all over again." He rubbed his chin and shook his head.

Car doors slammed in the parking lot, and then footsteps rushed through the lobby. We all looked in the direction of the sound to see who was coming. My fight or flight response had clearly not gotten the memo to calm down, and my body tensed up as I prepared to take the 'flight' option.

The tension in my shoulders released when I saw Aunt Lori racing down the aisle to me at a full gallop, with Pen Adams trying to keep up with her.

"Mandy-bel, what on earth happened?" she cried out as she shoved past Dylan and Jeremy to hug me tight.

Pen's gaze went directly to the light on the stage and stayed riveted to the sight. The color drained from his face. "Not again."

"I'm afraid so," Danny replied. Even dressed in the jeans and tee shirt he'd been wearing for dinner when he got the call, the police chief managed to maintain an air of authority. His eyes narrowed as he looked at Pen. "I have to ask, Mr. Adams, where were you this evening?"

Pen gestured gracefully toward Aunt Lori. "I was having dinner with this lovely lady."

"Really, Aunt Lori? I warned you to be careful," I whispered so Pen couldn't hear.

"And yet, here I am, perfectly fine. While you're the one who someone tried to kill tonight," she responded in a low tone.

She wasn't wrong.

A thought struck and I frowned. "How did you know to come here?"

"Jeremy called Pen to alert him to the situation. Since an attempt was made on your life, I'm graciously not going to point out I would've preferred to have learned about it from you."

"Sorry I didn't text, but I was a little busy running for my life." I paused and planted my tongue firmly in my cheek. "And thanks for *not* pointing it out."

The corners of her lips tilted up. "You're welcome. Seriously though, Mandy-bel, I'm so relieved you're safe."

More police officers arrived on the scene, and we were told to leave the stage. We all trooped down to the seating area of the theater and flopped in the front row. Jeremy on one side of me and Dylan on the other. I picked up Fluffy and put her in my lap, where she promptly put her chin on the arm rest of Dylan's seat and gazed up at him.

"Someone is besotted with you," I observed.

"Interesting as that information is, now is not the time for your confession, Amanda." Jeremy smirked.

Chief Carlow saved my best friend from getting socked in the arm by me when he raised his voice and said, "We have contact information for all of you, so you may leave for tonight."

"Do you want me to come home with you?" Aunt Lori asked, concern etched on her face.

I was a little tempted, but shook my head. "No, I'll be fine. Mom and Dad have an alarm system at the house. I don't usually use it, but I'll turn it on tonight. Plus, I've got my guard dog here." I patted Fluffy on the head, before placing her on the floor and standing.

"I'll follow you home and make sure everything is all right," Jeremy said.

"Me too," Dylan added.

"See. I'll be fine, Aunt Lori." I hugged my aunt and hissed in her ear, "You be safe too."

"He was with me when this happened. I'm perfectly safe with Pen," she whispered back, and then raised her voice to say, "I'm off in the morning, so I'll swing by your house with bagels and coffee. I'll text first, so you can turn off the alarm. I don't want Danny's breakfast to be disturbed by a false alarm, since he already missed dinner."

Her words about Pen being with her did calm me down about her being on yet another date with a murder suspect.

But as I drove home, with Jeremy's tail lights in front of my car, and Dylan's headlights behind me, I realized something. Aunt Lori was Pen's alibi for tonight, so in theory she was safe as houses with him. Unless, he was in cahoots with someone else and that person was the one who dropped the light tonight, while Pen was oh-so-conveniently out to dinner with my aunt.

I didn't think we could take Pen off the suspect list just yet after all.

Aunt Lori pulled into the driveway in her compact electric vehicle while I watered Mom's flowers out front. Fluffy stood staunchly at my side and barked. She hadn't left me for a second since we got home last night. My brave, little protector. She hadn't even wanted me to loop her leash on the wrought iron holder. Apparently, six feet away from me was six feet too many for her this morning.

"Shh, it's just Aunt Lori. We're safe."

Miraculously, Fluff understood and settled back down in the grass by my feet.

Aunt Lori exited the car, and called over her shoulder while she retrieved the bagels and coffee from the hatchback. "Should you be out here alone?"

"Asked the woman who had dinner and drinks with a murder suspect last night."

"You're such a wit," she said and slammed the hatch shut with her elbow since she had a huge sack of bagels in one hand and a cardboard caddy with four coffees in the other.

I turned off the hose and dropped it. I'd come back later to finish watering and would coil it up then. Hopefully, it wasn't visible on the doorbell camera, because my dad would pitch a fit if he saw me leaving the hose on the lawn.

"C'mon out to the deck. I thought it would be nice to sit out there today."

We strolled around the side of the house with Fluffy trotting right next to my ankle. I stumbled. She was seriously pressed up right against me.

"I see The Beast is still on guard duty," Aunt Lori said as we climbed the stairs to the back deck.

"No complaints here. Fluffy saved my life last night."

My aunt plopped the bag of bagels on the table, and handed me a coffee with 'Mandy-bel' printed on it.

"Please tell me you didn't use the name Mandy-bel at the Sit and Sip. Your nickname for me is supposed to be our little secret."

She took a sip of her coffee and sat in a shady spot under the umbrella. Aunt Lori was always very cautious about sun exposure, which is why she still had the porcelain complexion of a twenty-year old who'd always lived in an underground cave.

"Whatever. Have a bagel."

The bag crinkled as I opened it, and I inhaled the heavenly aroma of freshly baked bagels. The yeasty dough, a hint of garlic from the everything bagels. "How many people are you expecting? There has to be a dozen bagels in here."

"Hello!" Jeremy's voice called from the bottom of the stairs to the deck.

I looked in that direction to see Cara climbing the steps behind Jeremy.

"I may have invited Jeremy and Cara," Aunt Lori said.

"I guess I should've realized there are four coffees. Some amateur sleuth I am."

Cara pushed past Jeremy and rushed toward me, which

set Fluffy off in a frenzy of barking. I put my body between her and Cara and hugged my friend.

"I'm so relieved you're safe. I couldn't believe when Lori called this morning and told me what happened. By the way, why precisely did I have to hear it from your aunt?" She narrowed her eyes at me and frowned.

"I didn't want to call too late and disturb Mitch and the kids."

She waved her hands dismissively. "They'd fall back to sleep. I'm always here for you. *Tous pour un, un pour tous!*"

We all settled at the table, and I selected a bagel liberally coated with poppy seeds and promptly slathered it with cream cheese. Hey, if a girl couldn't splurge a little after a near death experience, when can she?

"Did Aunt Lori also tell you she had a romantic rendezvous with a potential killer last night? She went out with Pen Adams again."

Aunt Lori spread a scant amount of cream cheese on her sesame seed bagel. "He's a charming man. Plus, it seemed like a good opportunity to enjoy a nice dinner while seeing if I could learn anything about the murder from him."

"And did you?" Jeremy asked right before he took a huge bite of an everything bagel.

"Not too much over dinner," she admitted. "But we went for a nightcap at the bar in the Maple Hills Arms after we left the theater. Which by the way, is absolutely charming. It's designed to look like a 1920's speakeasy, and they serve amazing classic cocktails. I had the best sidecar last night. We all have to go sometime."

"It's great there, and count me in on the cocktails, but I'm more curious about what you found out from Pen Adams." Cara dug through the sack, pulled out a bagel, and waved it triumphantly in the air. "Salt! My favorite."

Aunt Lori put down her bagel and leaned forward in her seat. "Let me tell you, after the incident with Mandybel last night, Pen is worried about whether or not the show can go on."

Jeremy swallowed hastily. "I got a text from him this morning, saying he's called off rehearsal for today. And I heard from the theater's owner, who is worried they're going to pull out of the production." He turned to look at me. "And we're not supposed to go to the theater today, so I hope you didn't leave anything there. If you did, maybe Danny could send an officer to accompany you. Since, y'know, you're his future sister-in-law and all."

I think even my toes blushed at Jeremy's teasing comment. "I am not."

"Don't think I'm not dying to hear about the Dylan situation, because I so am, but what else did you learn from your date, Lori?" Cara said.

"I asked him if he'd lose a lot of money, as the producer, if the show didn't make it to Broadway. He said he has production insurance which will cover the costs. Without coming right out and saying it, I had the distinct impression he might even get a bigger payout from the insurance company than he'd need to pay off the cast and crew, etcetera."

"In other words, Pen will profit from the show not going on?" I asked.

Jeremy waggled one hand back and forth. "Maybe, maybe not. It depends on if it was a success. If *Agony in the Aspens* is a smash hit, I suspect he'd stand to earn a lot more money from it than he would from an insurance payout."

"Melville Dickens thinks the show is a stinker, and while he's not the most impartial observer, I have to agree it doesn't look good to me from what I've seen of rehearsals." I took a sip of my coffee, grateful for the caffeine, as I'd tossed and turned all night. I'd imagined every sound was the killer coming back to take another whack at me.

"It isn't the best show I've ever seen, but you never know what's going to strike the public's fancy," Jeremy said.

"And musicals are always popular with audiences," Cara added.

"Pen also told me there's another insurance policy." Aunt Lori paused and looked up at the sky and snapped her fingers. "What did he call it? It would be paid out to Hillner's survivors since he was killed on the job."

My years of human resources experience made my response automatic. "Worker's compensation."

Aunt Lori pointed at me. "That's it! And while it's not much money, he mentioned yet another insurance payout. This one from a life insurance policy. He didn't tell me how much it was, but I know from reading mysteries and listening to true crime podcasts, it could be a lot of money for the beneficiary."

"Who is probably Magdalena. Interesting. If we're looking at a financial motive, there's one right there," I said.

Jeremy scrunched up his face and shook his head. "I don't know, from the gossip I've heard from the crew, Magdalena is the one with the money. Her mother was a big Broadway star back in the day, and since her parents were divorced and she's an only child, she inherited everything when her mother died. She's loaded, and Aaron depended on her to support him. She even insisted he be brought on as the director for this production, otherwise he never would've gotten the gig."

"I wonder where Magdalena was last night?" I tapped my finger on my chin.

"She was at the inn. Pen called her to see if she wanted

to join us for drinks. And she did come downstairs. Said she'd fallen asleep in her room after dinner. Made it seem like it was because she was so grief-stricken."

"Did she seem grief-stricken to you?" I asked.

"She came downstairs in a chic black jumpsuit with red heels that made her over six feet tall. It might be her idea of mourning clothes, but she looked so glamorous, even I felt frumpy next to her, and feeling frumpy is not my jam," Aunt Lori said.

"I'd like to see the woman who could make you feel frumpy," Cara said, her eyes wide.

"Magdalena is gorgeous," I admitted. "But I don't really like her. With the possible financial motive for her, I was hoping you were going to say she crept downstairs dressed like a cartoon bandit in an outfit she could've worn for climbing around the rafters."

"She can't really prove she was sleeping alone in her room, but red stilettos are not designed for scrambling around over the stage. We need to think of other possibilities," Jeremy said.

After a pause while we all munched on our bagels, Cara said, "There are other motives besides money. As a parent, I have to say if Hillner was messing around with my daughter the way he was with Kaylee, I'd be on the warpath. I hate to think it's a local person, but Larry Tufton blamed you for not acting like a human chastity belt for Kaylee. I don't think we can rule him out as a suspect."

"Good point,'" Jeremy said. "And from the local pool of suspects, Caleb Symansky was furious at you too, Amanda. He might've been the one to try to harm you last night."

My delicious bagel was like sawdust in my suddenly dry mouth. I washed it down with a sip of coffee. "Thank you for laying out the vast array of people who might want to kill me. I've never felt so unpopular in my life, and growing up, we were total nerds. But, you're right. I need to see if either of them have alibis for last night. I wonder where they are today?"

Cara raised her hand. "I know where Caleb is. He's at the ball field coaching. Martin had a practice this morning."

"Larry's an accountant. I think he works in Hartford. I imagine he's at his office," Aunt Lori said.

"Good info, Aunt Lori." I turned to look at Cara. "Then Caleb, it is. Can I go with you to pick up Martin today, Cara? We can try to find out where Caleb was last night when the light almost dropped on my head."

Chapter Fourteen

Cara and I arrived at the field a short time before practice was due to end. We strolled over to the team, and I froze in my tracks and looked down at my shorts and tee shirt. I dressed to water the flowers and have breakfast with my aunt, and was under no illusion I was looking my best.

"You didn't tell me Dylan would be here."

"I didn't know. Danny is the coach, but he's been busy lately. I guess he couldn't make it, and Dylan is filling in for him. Such a good brother. I thought you'd be happy to see him." She looked me up and down, and plucked a leaf from my hair, which she held up for me to see before dropping it to the ground. "Oh, it's the outfit, huh? Don't worry about it, you look adorable. Very ... comfortable."

"Comfortable? Oh, yeah, that's precisely how I want Dylan to see me looking. Especially with nature in my hair from when I had to go through the bushes to wrestle with the hose."

I watched Dylan where he stood at third base, and

noticed the exact moment when he saw me. His face lit up, and he waved before trotting our way.

"I guess he digs the nature girl look you have going today," Cara said.

"Amanda! I'm so happy to see you. How are you feeling today?" He reached my side and leaned down to peck my cheek.

"Fine, just fine." I ran my hand through my hair in an effort to smooth it, and hopefully snag any other stray pieces of shrubbery still remaining in it. "We're here to pick up Martin. I didn't expect to see you."

"Yeah, I should be working at the orchard, but Danny needed me to take over the practice. After what happened to you last night, the investigation has gone into overdrive."

"I should hope so." Cara shuddered. "Our girl could've been killed last night."

Dylan pulled off his baseball cap and ran his hand through his hair. "Don't remind me. I don't think I slept a wink last night, worrying about it."

"I've had better nights' sleep myself," I admitted.

"What are you doing tonight?" Dylan asked.

"Setting the house alarm and locking myself in again. Pretty much my nighttime plans until this killer is caught. Why?"

"I was thinking when I finished work, I'd grab a pizza and swing by your place for dinner? What do you say?" he asked.

"I say I'll open a bottle of red."

"Great. Any topping preference?"

"Eggplant is my favorite," I said without hesitation.

He bobbed his head. "Noted. I'll text when I'm on my way. Probably around six o'clock?"

"Sounds good. Thanks, Dylan. I'll appreciate the company. And the pizza."

He flashed me a grin and then jogged back to the field to resume his coaching duties.

"You two are so stinking cute together. In my head, teenaged Cara is jumping up and down and squealing."

"Teenaged Amanda is a little bit too, but I have to tell you, the real-life grown-up version of Dylan is so much better than even my teenaged fantasy of him. I really like this guy." I gnawed on my bottom lip.

"So what's the problem? He's clearly into you too."

"I quit my career, sold my condo, and came back here to work at my writing. Not to get all caught up in a romance with my childhood heartthrob."

"Who says you can't do both?" Cara asked with a shrug. "You were always good at multitasking."

My heart sped up as I considered the possibility of writing and dating Dylan at the same time. "I could try to make it work, I guess. But first I've got to solve the mystery of who killed Hillner."

"And who's trying to kill you. Speaking of," Cara jerked her head toward the team bench. "There's Caleb now."

As soon as practice was over, Cara grabbed my arm and tugged me toward Caleb. The young man in question scowled at me as we approached, but Cara fixed a bright smile to her face and ignored it. "How's it going, Caleb?"

"I've been better, Ms. Diamond." The glare he sent my way left no room for doubt he blamed me for his troubles.

"I heard about Kaylee and you. I'm so sorry." Cara's smile faded to a sympathetic moue.

Honestly, she should've been the star of all of our high school plays. Who knew she was such an actress?

"I thought she'd come back to me, but she's not. Why just last night—"

"What happened last night?" I interrupted in a rush.

Cara kept her gaze focused on Caleb and managed to subtly smack me in the arm at the same time. Okay. Not my most smooth move, I admit. But we were here to talk to him about his whereabouts last night, and I got overexcited.

He cast a quizzical glance my way, but turned back to Cara and said, "She passed me on the road. I need to talk to her, and she's not taking my calls, so I followed her."

Stalker, much? Sheesh. I was starting to think Kaylee would be better off without this guy.

"You followed her where?" Even Cara's sympathetic façade slipped, and she scrunched up her nose, and her lips turned down at the corners.

"She went to the theater."

"The Theater in the Pines?" I bounced on the balls of my feet. Was he placing Kaylee at the scene of the crime last night?

He rolled his eyes so hard, his entire head lolled on his shoulders. "Of course the Theater in the Pines. What other theater is there in town?"

"Valid point," I conceded.

"Anyway, she was sitting in her car in the parking lot. I went to see what she was doing there."

"And what was she doing there? Nothing was sched-uled for volunteers last night." Unless you counted a volun-teer possibly trying to kill me, that is. But that was not on my official volunteer calendar.

"She said she wanted to feel close to Aaron Hillner, and it's where they used to meet." Unshed tears glistened in his eyes, and his voice broke.

"In the parking lot? Romantic." Cara snorted.

"I don't know what part of the theater they used to——" Caleb paused and waved his hands in the air. "I don't like to imagine it. But she said your car was there last night, and she didn't want to have to talk to anyone, so she just sat in her car and remembered him."

My eyes narrowed. "How did she know it was my car?"

"The California license plates. Duh."

"Oh right. I really need to get to the DMV and change those."

"Fascinating as your auto registration is, can we get back to Kaylee? What happened next?" Cara asked.

He shrugged. "Nothing, really. She decided to leave and come back later, when Ms. Seldon was gone. I asked if we could go to our spot to talk, but she shot me down. That's when I realized she wasn't coming back to me." His shoulders slumped.

Cara patted his arm. "You'll find someone else. Someone better."

"There's no one better than Kaylee. No one!" His hands clenched into fists, and Cara backed up a step.

"Do you know if she stayed at the theater?" I asked, ignoring the whole minefield of Caleb and Kaylee's relationship.

"I don't know. I haven't talked to her since then."

"Where did you go when you left the theater?" I asked. Was it possible Caleb had lingered after Kaylee left and snuck in to try to harm me, since he'd told me earlier he blamed me for Aaron and Kaylee's affair?

"I came here."

"The town sports fields? Why?" Cara asked,

"This was our spot."

Almost as romantic as the theater parking lot. Kaylee really needed to value herself more and find a better guy than Aaron or Caleb next time.

"How late did you stay here?" I asked.

"Late. It was after two o'clock when I got home. Why do *you* care?" His lip curled up as he looked at me like I was a piece of rotten fish on his dinner plate.

"Because someone tried to kill me last night at the theater. And you just admitted Kaylee and you were both there, and what's more, you both knew I was there." I put my hands on my hips and looked around the field. "Plus you just admitted you were out here, alone, with no corroborating witness."

He squinted. "What do you mean?"

"It means you have no alibi for the time the attack on me occurred. And Kaylee might not either." I made a mental note to hunt down Kaylee next to hear her side of the story.

"Don't you dare say anything bad about Kaylee." He put his hands on his hips and glared at me.

I held up my hands. "Cool down. I'm just trying to figure out who tried to harm me." And his hair trigger-temper did nothing to convince me he wasn't capable of it.

CARA DROPPED ME AT MY HOUSE, AND THEN WENT HOME, because the kids were having friends over to swim.

Fluffy was overjoyed to see me. Her claws clicked on the tile floor of the kitchen as she danced around me like Fred Astaire on speed. I scooped her up, and she whimpered with happiness as she licked my face.

"Flattering as this greeting is, I wasn't gone that long, Fluff."

I had left her home alone while Cara and I went on our sleuthing mission. I'd been planning to get my car and drive back to town to find Kaylee, but decided I better spend some time with Fluffy first.

After a couple of hours of research and work on the outline of my novel, Fluffy slept with her head on top of my feet under the kitchen table. She was comfortable, and to tell the truth so was I, but it was time to head into town.

I logged off my laptop, and looked down at Fluffy. I didn't have the heart to leave her alone again.

"Want to go bye-byes in the car?"

She lifted her head, and her whiskers were flattened where they'd been pressed to my foot. She stood, and the tags on her collar jingled as she shook and then trotted for the door.

"I'll take that as a yes."

While I waited for Fluffy to do her business outside, I called Aunt Lori. After a couple of pleasantries, I asked, "Do you have any idea where I might find Kaylee Tufton?"

"Funny you should ask. I just had a hair appointment, and she was at the salon getting a manicure. She was having those acrylic talons removed. Then she said she was going to the Sit and Sip. Why?"

"Turns out she was at the theater last night, and I want to find out where she was when the lighting equipment almost killed me."

"You can probably beat her to the Sit and Sip. Her nail appointment looked grueling, so she probably hasn't left the salon yet. Speaking of, I'd like to take you for a mani/pedi as a welcome home present. Does tomorrow work for you?"

"Sure. We can't do anything at the theater yet, so I've got plenty of time. Thanks, Aunt Lori."

"Great, I'll set up the appointment and text you the details. Now, you get to the Sit and Sip."

We ended the call, I hustled Fluffy along and into the

car, and we raced downtown. By some parking miracle, I found a spot on the street right in front of the Sit and Sip.

I lifted Fluffy out of the car and heard a voice behind me.

"Hi, Ms. Seldon."

I turned around, with Fluffy still in my arms, to see Kaylee emerge from the Sit and Sip with some sort of coffee drink with about six inches of whipped cream on top. Oh to be twenty-one again, when you could drink something so caloric and fat laden and not gain five hundred pounds.

"Hi, Kaylee. Can we talk for a minute?"

"Sure." She pointed to a small café table in front of the Sit and Sip. "Want to sit down?"

"Perfect."

Fluffy's body was stiff and tense in my arms, and I knew the hustle and bustle of Main Street had her anxious. And as an anxious Fluffy was a snappy Fluffy, I opted to hold her.

"I saw Caleb this morning."

"I'm sorry for you." Kaylee's jaw clenched. "He's behaving like an immature jerk lately."

"It seemed like he's having a hard time letting go."

"Is he ever. He was following me last night. Literally following me, like some kind of creepy stalker." Kaylee shuddered.

"He mentioned he saw you going to the theater and stopped to talk to you."

"Talk to me? More like harass me."

"I'm sorry it was an uncomfortable experience for you." I paused and added, "I was at the theater last night; you should've come in to say hello."

"I wanted to be alone. Y'know, in my grief." She

slurped her beverage and ended up with a whipped cream mustache, which she swiped off her lip with her tongue.

"Right. Of course." I bobbed my head. "Then where did you go, if you decided not to come into the theater?"

"I just went home."

It occurred to me I could get two birds with one stone and determine Larry Tufton's whereabouts also. "Then you didn't get to be alone in your grief after all. You live with your parents, don't you?"

"I do, but Mom had her book club meeting, and Dad is never there. He works in the city, and it's always really late by the time he gets home. Mom handles everything with the house and family, which is why it was so ridiculous the way he overreacted to my relationship with Aaron. I mean, if he really cared, maybe he could've tried being there for me just once in my entire life."

"It sounds rough." I honestly had no clue what to say to her. I mean, she was having an affair with a much older, married man who ended up murdered, and there were more suspects than the population of some small towns. I think her dad had a right to be a little flipped out about it. Although, his behavior toward me did seem out of bounds.

"You have no idea. But at least I had the house to myself until Mom got home around ten."

"Wow, your dad wasn't home from work at ten o'clock at night?"

"Nope. He got home about fifteen minutes after Mom did."

"That's a really long day for him."

"It was a little later than usual, now that you mention it. He's usually home by around eight or eight thirty."

"Did he say why he was so late?" I asked.

"I'm not speaking to him. Why do you care about him

being late? I can't imagine he's your favorite person either, after the way he spoke to you."

"I'm just being nosy, I guess."

What I was really doing was trying to figure out where Larry Tufton was between eight and ten fifteen that night. It seemed highly suspicious to me the man who blamed me for his daughter's affair with Aaron Hillner was missing in action at just the precise time someone tried to murder me.

Chapter Fifteen

B *loop*. My phone alerted me someone was at the front door. My heart rate kicked up a notch. It was probably Dylan with the pizza. Or, the way things have been going since I hit town, it was possibly someone trying to kill me. Fingers crossed it was the former. I picked up my phone from the kitchen counter and tapped on the app to view the camera. It was Dylan, holding a pizza box. If it wasn't two of my favorite fantasies right there, I don't know what was.

Maybe a celebrity with a giant check, telling me I won a sweepstakes contest. Or a literary agent begging to represent my work, also with a giant check. Dylan with a pizza was only slightly more realistic than those two fantasies. I still couldn't believe he and I had a mutual attraction to each other.

Fluffy chased me to the door, her barks echoing in the hallway. "Shh, Fluff. It's just Dylan. You like Dylan, remember?"

My pup didn't believe me, and her barking increased in volume and franticness as we got closer to the front door.

I held her back with my bare foot, as I opened the door. "Hi, Dylan. Hush."

"Okay, I'll hush." The corners of his mouth tilted up, and his hazel eyes twinkled.

"The 'hush' was for Fluffy."

He looked down at the shih tzu, who had stopped the ferocious barking but now made little yips of pleasure as she danced around his feet. "Fluffy and me are old friends. Right, girl?"

"Let me take the pizza box, so you can greet her. She's not going to calm down until you do. There is nothing more stubborn than a shih tzu." I took the box out of his hands, and the delectable aroma of yeasty crust, garlic, and tomato sauce wafted up to my nose. My eyes fluttered shut. "This smells so good."

Dylan squatted and petted Fluffy, who put her front paws on his knees and licked his face. I'd never seen her behave this way with anyone but me. I firmly believed dogs had sound instincts about people, so it made me happy Dylan clearly met with her wholehearted approval.

"I got half pepperoni and half eggplant. My favorite and your favorite. It seemed like a good compromise." He smiled up at me while Fluffy continued her frantic greeting.

"It all sounds good to me. Your pepperoni might not be safe." I started to walk down the hallway to the kitchen, and called over my shoulder. "Fluffy, let the man come to the kitchen and eat his dinner."

I put the pizza box on the granite island and turned to face Dylan, who looked around with curiosity. "I've seen the outside of your folks house across the pond from the orchard, but I've never been in it before. It's very nice."

"They updated the kitchen recently, so it's very different from when I lived here before. But the rest of the house is pretty much the same. Right down to the posters on the wall in my bedroom."

He laughed, and the deep, rich sound caused a flutter in my tummy. "How long are you going to be in town? Long enough to take down the posters?"

"Oh, the posters are down. First thing I did after I unpacked." I opened a white cabinet and reached for two plates.

Dylan stepped to my side and took them from me. "Are we eating at the kitchen table?"

"Yes. It's a nice night, but the deck has too many mosquitos at this time of year to be a comfortable place to eat dinner. I think it's the proximity to the pond. It's like a mosquito breeding ground out there."

He placed the dishes on the table, and grabbed two napkins out of the holder on the center of the table. The one I'd made in my middle school woodworking class. He chuckled. "I have this same napkin holder in my house."

"I guess we all made them. Woodworking was a required class, so probably every house in town has the same one." I laughed, and grabbed a wine glass for me. "Wine? Or would you prefer something else? There's beer, fizzy water, soda, or hard cider in the fridge."

"I might try a cider. I've been looking into what we need to do to start a cider brewing operation at the orchard, so I'm interested in what other companies are making."

I grabbed a frosty beer mug from the freezer, and the cider from the fridge, and Dylan strolled over to take each from me. As he poured his cider in the mug, I took a wine glass out of a cupboard and poured a glass of the red I'd opened right before Dylan arrived.

"Trying to diversify?" I held out my wine glass and

Dylan tore his attention from the cider label he'd been studying and we clinked glasses.

"Cheers. And, yeah. The fall is always a busy time with leaf peepers, and even locals. But we really depend on the fall sales to sustain us all year. It would be nice to have a more year-round revenue source like the hard cider."

I opened a drawer and pulled out a pizza wheel with a bright, red handle. "Why don't you have a seat, and we can dig in while the pizza is hot."

We sat down, and Dylan used the pizza wheel to remove a piece of the eggplant and put it on my plate. Abundant mozzarella stretched out as he separated the slice. My mouth watered at the sight of the pieces of breaded and fried eggplant nestled into the gooey, melted cheese.

As we began to eat our pizza, a pathetic whimper sounded from beneath the table.

"I don't think pizza is good for dogs," Dylan said.

"It's not. And no matter how big and sad those brown eyes get, don't let her convince you I'm starving her. She had her dinner before you got here. She's just hoping for a piece of pepperoni to fall from the sky into her mouth." I craned my neck to look under the table and address my next comment to Fluffy. "And I don't know why, because it has never once happened. You are nothing if not persistent, oh-fluffy-one."

OVER DINNER THE CONVERSATION FLOWED, JUST LIKE IT had at the diner the other night. We talked about everything except the murder, which was fine by me. I wanted the chance for Dylan and me to get to know each other better, and not just our youthful images of each other.

He wadded up his napkin and tossed it on the table. "That was delicious."

"If you have room, I did pick up some ice cream from We've Got the Scoop."

His eyes gleamed. "There's always room for ice cream. What flavor did you get?"

"My favorite is the Toffee Caramel Dream, so I got a small container of it, and I didn't know what you liked, so I got a chocolate-vanilla swirl, because I figured everyone likes one or the other of those two flavors."

"The toffee is one of my favorites too, and I like the chocolate-vanilla swirl. So they're both excellent choices, but their bing cherry vanilla tops out my list. If you like cherry, you should try it sometime."

"Bing cherry vanilla is my second favorite, as a matter of fact." Yet another thing we had in common. Our lives had taken very different paths, with me moving to two of the biggest cities in the country to live and make my career, and Dylan coming back home to run the family business, but we were on the same page about so many things, it was kind of freaky.

"Why don't we do a combo of the two?" he suggested.

"Good idea, then we both get some toffee."

As I got down the bowls and began to scoop the ice cream into them, Dylan asked from the table. "When are your parents due back from their trip?'

"They'll be back sometime in the fall. It's such a pretty time of year here, they didn't want to miss it."

He grimaced. "I don't really get to enjoy the fall foliage too much. It's my busy season. I'm on the go from dawn until I collapse into bed at night."

I stuck a spoon in each bowl and carried them to the table.

"If you're looking for help in the fall, my position at the

theater will be done, and I'll be in need of another part-time job."

"Good to know. We can always use help. The shop is always busy."

"You know, until I moved away from Maple Hills, I didn't realize every town didn't have a shop that sold apples and maple sugar candy."

"You mean LA isn't filled with super-sweet candy shaped like maple leaves?" He winked at me before shoving a huge spoonful of ice cream in his mouth."

"Nope."

We enjoyed our dessert for a few moments; the only sound was when our spoons clinked on our bowls.

Dylan swallowed his last spoonful and asked, "So you plan on still being here in the fall? I wasn't sure what you were going to do when your folks got home."

"I'm here for the foreseeable future. Although, when my parents get home, I'm thinking about looking for my own place. There are those new townhomes by the lake, and I was thinking one of those might be a good investment."

"They're nice, but a little pricey."

"Not compared to LA real estate. I sold my condo there at the height of a boom, so I could buy one of these for just a fraction of what my place was worth there. It's wild what people are willing to pay in southern California for even the tiniest of homes."

"I'm glad to know you'll be staying, although I'll miss knowing you're right across the pond from my house."

I chuffed out a breath. "Not to bring up the conversational elephant in the room we've been avoiding all night, but if the murder isn't solved by the fall, I might just stay with my folks. I feel safer here with the Rosenbergs right next door, and my parents' state-of-the-art alarm system."

"Danny will catch the killer, don't you worry."

"I hope so. Has he talked to you about the case? Do you know if he's making any progress?"

"He never discusses police business with me, but he's a good cop. I have every confidence in him. Do you still feel like you need to be conducting your own investigation?"

"It's not a formal investigation or anything, but I'm still asking around. And I will be as long as your brother has me on his suspect list."

"I'm sure you're way down at the bottom of his suspect list. A footnote, even. Especially since the attempt was made on your life."

"Which is another reason I'm going to keep at it. If someone is out to get me, I'm not going to just pull the covers over my head and hide. I'm going to find them and stop them."

"I get it, and I admire you for your determination, but I'll be glad when Danny has someone under arrest."

"Someone who's not me." I waved my spoon at him.

One side of his mouth quirked up, revealing a dimple. "That goes without saying."

My phone pinged from the charger on the counter. "Sorry, I'm expecting to hear from Aunt Lori." I stood up and retrieved my phone. I leaned my backside against the counter while I read the text.

"Is everything okay with Lori?"

I nodded. "Yes. She offered to take me to Shear Madness for some pampering tomorrow as a welcome home present, and I am not too proud to accept a free mani/pedi. And she said we have an eleven a.m. appointment. Phew, it's not too early."

He looked at the clock on the wall over my head. "Oh wow, I hadn't realized it was so late. I should get going. I have an early morning tomorrow." He flashed a rueful grin my way. "Who am I kidding, when you own and operate an apple orchard, every morning is an early morning."

I shoved my phone in my back pocket and picked up Fluffy from the floor. "We'll walk you out. It can double as Fluffy's last trip outside for the night."

He stood and glanced at the pizza box and plates on the table. "I can stay and help you clean up."

"No worries. You brought dinner, which is sort of like cooking. And I think if one person cooks, then the other can do the dishes. It's how my parents always did things."

"Sounds like a fair deal, thanks."

I grabbed Fluffy's leash off the table next to the front door and clipped it to her collar. Once we were outside, I placed her on the grass. Rather than walking to his truck, Dylan came and stood beside us.

His lips formed a straight line as he peered into the trees on the side of our house. "It's kind of isolated here."

I jerked my thumb over my shoulder toward the comforting glow of lights in the windows at the neighboring house. "Mr. and Mrs. Rosenberg are right over there."

"I guess, but if you wanted I could stay here tonight."

I hesitated. "Thanks, but I don't think we're at the sleepover stage yet. I'd like to take things slow and get to know each other better."

His eyes opened wide, and he held up his hands. "I am totally on board with the going slow thing. I'm sorry I wasn't clear. It wasn't a come-on. I meant I could sleep on the sofa or something, so you wouldn't be alone in this big house."

"It's really sweet of you to offer, but I'm not alone. I've got Fluffy. And the alarm system. We'll be fine."

"Are you sure? Because I don't mind."

Fluffy squatted on the grass next to me. "I'm positive.

She'll be all set until morning now, so we won't need to come outside again. When you leave, we're going to go inside, set the alarm, do the dishes, and then go to bed."

He held his thumb and forefinger a smidgeon apart. "Can I make one amendment to your plan?"

"Depends what it is." I picked up Fluffy.

"How about I wait until you're inside and the alarm is set."

"Okay, if it will make you feel better, but Fluff and I have been taking care of ourselves for a long time now."

"But not with a killer after you."

My pulse rate raced. "True. I'll give you the thumbs-up from the living room window when the alarm is set. Thanks."

"Actually, I do have one more potential amendment to the plan, if you're willing. A good night kiss?"

Now my heart pounded for another reason. Up until now, we'd only shared very chaste pecks on the cheek, and some hand holding.

"I'm willing to accept this amendment also." Internally I rolled my eyes. Contract negotiation jokes? I needed to improve my sexy banter.

"Good," Dylan put his hands on my shoulders and bent down to press his lips to mine.

He tasted like pizza and ice cream and Dylan, and I relaxed into the kiss until I might've even forgotten his brother suspected me of murder and an actual murderer was trying to kill me. I might've even rethought my no-sleepover rule, but Fluffy grunted and squirmed where she was pressed between us, and our moment of passion devolved into laughter.

"I guess Fluffy is ready to call it a night," I said.

Dylan rested his forehead against mine for a moment,

before straightening up to his full height. "Fluffy really does rule the roost here, doesn't she?"

I chuckled as I carried the canine dictator in question to the front door. I paused in the doorway to say, "You have no idea. Good night, Dylan. Thanks for a lovely evening."

Chapter Sixteen

Shear Madness was the salon we had all gone to back in the day, being as it was the only game in town. I walked in expecting it to look the same way it had when I was eighteen, but it had undergone a major renovation since the last time I'd been there. It was way more upscale and had a serious spa vibe working.

One thing that hadn't changed was the staff, or at least some of the staff. I saw the owner, Gina Gallo holding court at her hair station. She currently didn't have a client, but sat in the chair sipping coffee and talking to the other stylists' clients.

I waved when I spotted Aunt Lori already seated at a manicure station. The manicurist who sat across from her was familiar, but I struggled to remember her name. I've never been able to keep a manicure nice. It always seems to be chipped within minutes of leaving the salon, so I never had much interaction with her.

Unlike with Gina, who had cut my hair for years. She thumped her coffee mug down on her station and held her hands over her heart. "Are my eyes deceiving me, or is it Amanda Seldon, back in Maple Hills?"

"It's me, Gina." I strolled over, but she jumped up and met me halfway.

She was a petite woman, but she was wiry and strong, and the hug she gave me took my breath away. "Welcome home."

"It's good to be home."

"Are you here for your hair?" She wrinkled her nose and ran her fingers through my shoulder-length brown hair.

Okay, it had been a while since my last appointment. Getting ready to move had taken all my time and energy. Perhaps it was a little longer than shoulder length now, and the highlights could use a touch-up. "I'm here for a mani/pedi with Aunt Lori, but I'll make an appointment for my hair soon."

"Good, good." The dark hair of her precision-cut bob swung as she nodded her head. "Don't wait much longer."

I held up one hand. "I swear. Soon."

She beamed at me. "Now head on back to your aunt."

The other women in the salon, both patrons and employees, cast openly curious glances at me as I walked past to reach Aunt Lori.

"Hiya, Mandy-bel. Have a seat." She patted the chair at the manicure station next to hers. "You remember Sharon, right? She just finished my manicure, and she'll do yours now that you're here. And then we can move to the pedicure stations. You can go first there, because I'm always in heaven between the massage chair and the lovely, warm foot soak. I don't mind waiting."

Sharon was the woman's name, of course. "Hi, Sharon. I have to warn you, my nails are a disaster. I just packed up my place in LA to put everything in storage, and my fingernails were a major casualty of the process."

She took the hands I extended and tsked her tongue. "You aren't kidding. We've got our work cut out for us."

Aunt Lori wagged a finger. "And don't let the story about packing boxes fool you. Her nails are always a mess."

Busted. My face heated. "It's the truth. I am incapable of keeping a manicure looking nice."

"We'll do what we can. But you might want to consider a weekly appointment." Sharon stuck my fingertips in a shallow bowl of liquid. "Nourishing oils. And boy, do you need them, those are some dry cuticles. Soak for a bit. What can I get you to drink?"

I noticed Aunt Lori had a green bottle of fizzy water on her table, and I gestured to it with my head, since my hands were otherwise engaged. "I'll have one of those, thanks."

When Sharon had stepped into the back of the salon, Aunt Lori turned to me and said, "I went out with Pen again last night."

"You did? Please tell me you're being cautious."

"Mandy-bel, you don't make as many trips around the sun as I have without learning a few things. It's okay. We just had cocktails and charcuterie at the inn. He's good company, so charming."

"He is both of those things," I conceded. I lowered my voice and added, "And quite possibly a killer."

"I don't think he is, and I have good instincts about people."

Which was true. Aunt Lori was a shrewd judge of character, except where her ex-husband was concerned, which is why I was anxious about her spending time with Pen. Maybe romantic partners were an area where my otherwise savvy aunt had a blind spot. But there was no way I could ever say it to her, so I just made a noncommittal, humming sound.

After a brief silence Lori asked, "How are things going with Dylan? He was at your house for dinner when I texted last night, wasn't he?"

All sound in the salon stopped at her question, and I sensed everyone's eyes burning into me, even without looking at them. Their curiosity was palpable. "He brought over a pizza for us. It was delicious."

"I bet he's delicious," Gina called out from the front of the salon, and everyone laughed.

"Not Dylan, the pizza." My face heated up.

Sharon returned and put my water down. She sat in her seat and pulled out one of my hands. "I find it hard to believe Dylan Carlow isn't delicious, when he looks so edible."

Titters greeted her pronouncement.

Seriously? Sharon was old enough to be Dylan's mom. I squirmed in my seat.

Aunt Lori noticed my discomfort with the conversational direction and said, "You have to excuse everyone, Mandy-bel. But Dylan is a hot property here in town. Single, owns his own business—"

"Hotter than this contraption," an older lady with foil on her hair chortled, and pointed up at the heat lamp over her head.

Gina strolled back and sat next to Sharon and opposite Aunt Lori. "And he doesn't date much, which seems like such a waste."

"And it's not from a lack of effort on the part of the female population," Sharon added.

"True, lots of women have pursued him, and he even lets one catch him every now and again. But you're the first one we've seen him pursue." Gina leaned toward me. "What's your secret?"

All the attention was uncomfortable for me, as I was not an extroverted person by nature, but I couldn't deny this conversation just got really interesting to me. "I am?" I glanced at Aunt Lori for confirmation.

She nodded. "You are."

"Huh." I leaned against the back of my seat, and Sharon yanked my hand back toward her.

A woman getting her hair cut called out, "I heard a different story the other day. That you were carrying on with the married man who got himself killed at the Theater in the Pines."

"That is 100 percent false." I spoke louder than I intended to.

"I heard it too," a woman who'd entered the salon during this ridiculous conversation said.

Gina stood up to go help the new customer, and called over her shoulder, "I heard the same story. It's why Chief Carlow has you on his suspect list."

"You were living together in Los Angeles while his wife was back home in New York," the woman under the heat lamp added.

"Also not true. We were both living in Los Angeles, but I never met him until I came to Maple Hills. And I didn't much like him, either."

"Ixnay on the not-liking talk," Aunt Lori hissed at me.

The woman Gina was checking in said, "Word around town is you liked him a lot in Los Angeles, but when you got here and found out he was married *and* carrying on with other women too, you turned against him."

"I don't know how I can convince you guys. I never knew Hillner in Los Angeles, I wasn't carrying on an affair with him, and while I didn't like him, I certainly didn't feel strongly enough about him to murder him."

Heat-lamp woman would not be deterred. "My neighbor told me the Carlow brothers almost came to blows over Danny's suspicions of you in Hillner's murder."

"What? Absolutely not." A fine sheen of sweat formed at my hairline. These stories were getting worse and worse. The way talk was spiraling into increasingly outlandish stories, pretty soon, the town was going to be saying I knew where Jimmy Hoffa was buried because of my alleged mob connections.

"It would make sense if Dylan did defend you to his brother, because I heard someone say they heard from another person Dylan and you confessed your love for each other on Main Street. Right in front of the Sit and Sip. Word is he told you he's worshipped you his whole life," Gina said.

Boy, I had forgotten how the small town gossip mill worked. And if anything, this topic was worse than the one where everyone in town thought I was a murdering mistress. "Um, not quite. There was no mention of the 'L' word, or worshipping of any sort." I looked around at all the avid faces staring back at me. "Seriously. We were in the same grade all through school, so of course we knew of each other."

"And you had a crush on him," Aunt Lori said.

I glared at her, and she shrugged. "Sorry, but everyone knew it. You were adorable about him. And what I heard in the library was he admitted to you he had a crush on you too, back in high school. But not the worshipping-love thing."

"Aww." A collective swoon sounded throughout the salon.

I took a deep breath. "Your version is much closer to the truth than the worship story."

Gina threw back her head and laughed, a deep, throaty sound. "And whose going to worship you with that hair? I'm putting you on the books for tomorrow morning at ten thirty. Can you be here?"

I glanced at my reflection in the mirror behind Sharon. Gina was right, my hair needed help. "I'll be here."

LUCKILY, ONCE SHARON GOT INTO MY MANICURE, THE REST of the salon settled down, and dropped the talk about me killing Hillner and Dylan worshipping me.

According to Aunt Lori's plan, Sharon had done my pedicure first. While she worked on Aunt Lori's feet, I enjoyed the massage chair and stretched out my legs to admire my lilac-painted toenails while they dried.

Sharon spoke while she clipped my aunt's toenails. "Are you really gonna run off to New York with that producer fella when he goes back to the city?"

"Of course not. Where did you hear such a thing?" Aunt Lori sat up straight and lifted her nose in the air.

"Oh, now you look indignant when the gossip is about you." A bubble of laughter formed in my chest, and I couldn't hold it back if I tried. I was just so happy not to be on the hot seat anymore, I didn't even care if it took my beloved aunt jumping into the frying pan to make it happen. Besides, gossip about her whirlwind romance with a hotshot theater producer was a lot more flattering than the stories about me being some sort of bloodthirsty femme fatale.

"People talk in here." Sharon shrugged.

"We're just enjoying each other's company while Pen is

in town. I don't know if we'll see each other again when he leaves, but I most decidedly will not be leaving Maple Hills to be with him after knowing him for one week." Aunt Lori raised her voice, so all the eavesdroppers could hear her loud and clear.

"He's a good-looking guy for an older man, and I hear he's loaded," Sharon said.

"He is both of those things." Aunt Lori inclined her head. "But my niece just got back to town, and I'm enjoying her company too much to rush off and leave her."

My heart expanded at her words. "That's so sweet, Aunt Lori. I'm enjoying being with you too."

"What color do you want on your toes?" Sharon asked.

"That scarlet one I like for my toes." Lori wiggled her pale pink fingernails at me. "I like a subtle fingernail, and a flashy color for my toes."

"Gotcha." Sharon stood up and dried her hands on a towel. "I'm gonna go grab it. Be right back."

I lowered my voice so the whole world couldn't hear. "I'm glad you're not getting too serious with Pen. Potential murderer aside, do you two have much in common?"

"Under his urbane veneer, he's a nice guy. The conversation between us never lags. For instance, did you know he's known Magdalena since she was a little girl? He's like an honorary uncle to her, so he understands how special my relationship with you is."

My eyes widened, and I turned my head to look at Lori. "I didn't know he's been friends with her for so long. I assumed they just knew each other through work, since they're co-producers of *Agony in the Elms*."

"They've known each other for ages. He's always been a big-time theater producer, and her mother was a

Broadway star. According to Pen, she was a major musical performer. They were friends."

"Interesting. Friends or more than friends?" I asked.

"Just friends. She was married to Magdalena's father when they met. He was a stagehand." She corrected herself, "Well, the stage manager, according to Pen. Her dad started as a stagehand and worked his way up to stage manager."

"I can't imagine Magdalena as a little girl. She's so sophisticated. I sort of imagined she emerged fully grown from some posh Manhattan night club."

"I know, right? I said something similar to Pen, but he said she was an adorable little girl. She idolized her father. Her parents worked on the same show for a long time, one that Pen produced. He said she would be at the theater every chance she got. She'd scramble right up into the rafters with her dad." She chuckled and took a sip of her fizzy water. "Pen said, appearance to the contrary, she could probably do every job on the crew if she had to, because her whole childhood was like a stage craft apprenticeship."

"Really? Magdalena Hillner? We're talking about the same person, aren't we? Tall, exotic, kind of snotty?"

Sharon returned, shaking a bottle of nail polish. "Are we talking about the murdered guy's wife? She's a piece of work."

"You know her?" I asked.

"Uh-huh. She's a high maintenance sort, so she's been in here. Although, she made it perfectly clear she was slumming compared to the salons she's used to." She sat back down on her low stool, and swiped a coat of polish on Lori's big toe.

"How rude," Aunt Lori said.

"Rudeness we can take. You can't work in this business

without developing a thick hide, but she was a lousy tipper." Sharon smiled up at each of us in turn. "It's been nice seeing your friendly faces, let me tell you. I needed it after this morning."

"Bad morning?" I asked with a moue of sympathy. Working with the public could be brutal, even in a friendly place like Shear Madness.

"You betcha. That Hillner woman came in here for a manicure. A full set of acrylic nails."

"That's a big job," Aunt Lori said.

Sharon nodded. "It is. Expensive too, and she gave me like a one percent tip. I mean, have you ever heard of anything so stingy in your life?"

"It's more insulting than not tipping at all," I observed.

"You're right." Sharon waved the nail polish brush at me. "She was here when the doors opened, and I agreed to fit her in, thinking it would be a nice tip. But, no way. I worked on her for hours, between soaking off the old nails and putting on the new. And she didn't even need a full set. Only one was broken, I could've just replaced it. But she insisted, she wanted a new color." She picked up the bright red bottle of polish she was using on Aunt Lori and waggled it. "This one."

"Scarlet nails for the merry widow, huh?" Aunt Lori asked.

Sharon chuffed out a laugh. "It seemed a little inappropriate to me too. I mean the shade she had on was very on-trend. A nice neutral beige. With the long, pointed nails she had, it's super chic. With the scarlet on those long nails, and her pitch black hair, she looked like Vampira."

I stopped breathing, and Aunt Lori and I exchanged a pointed glance. "Let me be sure I understand, Magdalena was missing one of her long, pointy, beige nails, and insisted on an early morning appointment to get a full-set of a totally different color?"

"That about sums it up." Sharon completed the first coat of Lori's toes and started on the second.

"Aunt Lori, I hate to cut into our mani/pedi time, because I really appreciated this gift so much, but—"

"But you've got to go talk to Chief Carlow. I understand. Go!" She shooed me away.

I jumped up and kissed her on the cheek. "Thanks, Aunt Lori."

"What's happening?" Sharon asked. "Was it something I said?"

"It sure was." I pulled the generous tip I'd allocated out of the top of my tote bag, careful not to smudge my nails, and left it on the tray Sharon used for her pedicure equipment. "You provided a piece of information which just might help me catch the real killer and clear my name."

Chapter Seventeen

I raced down the street as fast as the flip-flops I'd worn for my pedicure today would allow. Which wasn't very. On the way, I called Dylan on my phone. He answered on the second ring.

"Hey, Amanda. How was the pampering?"

"Illuminating."

There was a brief pause, before Dylan replied in a puzzled voice, "I've never heard anyone describe a manicure as illuminating before."

I dodged a kid on a skateboard on the sidewalk, as I waited in front of the inn for the light to change, so I could cross the street. "It wasn't the manicure that was illuminating, it was the conversation. Do you know where your brother is?"

"Danny? Why? Was the illuminating conversation about the murder?"

"Yes, Danny. And possibly. I think I might've figured out who killed Aaron Hillner." I realized I'd raised my voice to be heard above the roar of a delivery truck on the street, and lowered it. "I really need to talk to Danny. Do you know where he might be? Or could I have his number?"

"Who is it?"

"I don't want to say until I've talked it over with Danny. Maybe I'm way off base, and I'd like to be sure before I start slandering someone's name."

"Okay, I get it. And, I can tell you both things you want to know. We just had lunch together, and he told me he was going to be at the theater this afternoon. He wanted to examine the scene of the crime again. And maybe talk to some of the crew, if they were around. And here's his number..." He reeled off a series of numbers.

"I'll never remember the number. I'm walking on Main Street right now. Would you mind texting it to me?"

"Sure. I'll do it right now."

"Thanks, Dylan. I think I might just head over to the theater to see if I can catch him."

The light changed, and I stepped off the curb to cross the street.

"Be careful, Amanda. If you've figured out who the killer is, you could be in serious danger."

"You know, more people have said that to me in the week I've been home in sleepy, little Maple Hills than in all the years I lived in Los Angeles."

He chuckled, and even over the speaker on my phone, the sound warmed me from within. "It's been an eventful time here in Maple Hills. I've managed to live my whole life here without ever warning someone they might be in danger. But still, be safe, okay?"

"I will be. Besides, I'm going to meet your brother, the police chief. What could possibly go wrong? I'm at my car now, I'll call you later."

I tapped at my nails gently with my fingertips before I dug through my purse for my keys. Good, it seemed like the quick-dry top coat Sharon used had really done the job. They were completely set. I pulled out my car keys, and heaved a deep sigh. I had my car keys, and the keys to my parents' house with me, but not the key I needed to get into the theater. Which, I was ninety-nine percent certain I'd need, as rehearsals were called off for today. The chief seemed to think crew members would be there today, so maybe I'd missed some kind of announcement about the play preparations recommencing, but better safe than sorry.

Arriving at the theater without my keys was a risk I wasn't willing to take. You didn't get to be the VP of Human Resources at a major corporation at thirty-five by not planning ahead. I'd just run home and grab my keys. Maybe Fluffy too, she'd been alone for a while and would probably enjoy the outing.

Not to mention, I'd feel a little safer with Fluffy at my side. I loved my girl, but I wasn't blind to her personality quirks, and there was a reason everyone called her The Beast.

GRAVEL CRUNCHED UNDER THE TIRES AS FLUFFY AND I rolled up to the Theater in the Pines. It looked like I'd beaten the chief here, because there were no cars in the parking lot.

I pulled out my phone and called the number Dylan had given me. It was Danny's personal number, so I'd hoped I could reach him more easily from it than the number at the police station, but no such luck. It went directly to voice mail. I left him a quick message, not going into too much detail but saying I'd meet him at the theater and I had some information for him.

"We might as well wait inside for the chief," I said to Fluffy.

Because, yes, I am that person who talks to their dog like she's a human being. But you can't convince me Fluffy doesn't understand every word I say to her. She may choose to disobey me, because she is a shih tzu, and they are the most single-minded creatures on the planet, but she always understands me.

Fluffy trotted up the steps by my side, panting happily as she looked around. When we got to the door, I shifted the leash from my right hand to my left, so I could use the old-fashioned key in the lock. I froze in place.

"Shoot. I forgot about the alarm, we probably should've used the stage door, so I could deactivate it right away."

To prove my earlier point about her always under-standing, Fluffy trotted toward the end of the porch, as if to walk around the building to the stage door in the rear. She stopped when she ran out of leash.

"Wait a minute, girl. I just remembered. Jeremy told me you can still come in at the front; you have three minutes to get to the back of the theater and turn off the alarm. When we get inside, I'm going to drop your leash and bolt for the back, okay?"

Her plumed tail wagged in agreement over her back.

I shut the door behind us and left it unlocked, because my goal was to keep Fluffy inside, not to keep anyone else, like the chief, outside.

"Okay, three minutes to get to the alarm." I took a deep breath and squinted into the dimly lit theater, which looked even darker after the bright summer sunshine outside. Dropping Fluffy's leash, I took off at a sprint down the left aisle of the theater.

The rubber soles of my flip-flops squeaked on the

wooden floor. Fluffy decided it was an excellent game and nipped playfully at my heels. I had to slow down for the stairs, and Fluffy got ahead of me. She pranced on the stage, barking happily, as if to say *C'mon, Mom! Let's go, let's go, let's GO!*

I trotted past her and made for the wings of the stage and zigzagged around crates and set pieces to get to the alarm pad by the stage door. I reached it with a little time to spare and pressed the code in as fast as I could.

Out of breath, I really did need to incorporate exercise into my day more, I leaned over and panted. Fluffy danced around me, yipping. She enjoyed the race through the dark theater, even if I didn't. We'd have to start taking walks around the neighborhood; it would be good for both Fluffy and me.

After I caught my breath, I strolled back to the stage, put my hands on my hips and surveyed the theater. Still no Chief Carlow, or Danny, as I had to get used to calling him, now that I was dating his brother.

"I guess I might as well try to get some work done before Danny gets here. Let's go to my office, girlie." I bent down to unclip Fluffy's leash and let her follow me on her own to my office.

We retrieved my tote bag from where I'd dropped it in the lobby, and entered my office. Once there, Fluffy flopped into her bed with a deep sigh of contentment and promptly closed her eyes.

I pulled my laptop out of the tote bag and turned it on to check my email to see if I'd heard from any more volunteers about the schedule. As I waited for it to boot up, I checked my phone to see if I had a message from the Chief. Nope.

As soon as I'd gotten into my email, the creak of one

of the front doors sounded, and sunlight poured into the lobby.

"Chief ... er, Danny ... is that you?" Maybe once he didn't suspect me of murder, calling him Danny would come more easily for me. But right now, he was still Chief Carlow, whom I had to convince I was most emphatically not a killer.

"No, it's me. Surprise."

I jumped at the sound of Magdalena Hillner's voice.

Oh no. The woman I had strong reason to believe had murdered her very own husband stood in the doorway of my office, with a most unpleasant smile on her face.

Alone in a dark, empty theater with a murderer. My day had definitely taken a turn for the worse.

AT THE SOUND OF ANOTHER PERSON'S VOICE, FLUFFY lifted her head and barked.

"Shut your little rat of a dog up," Magdalena snapped.

"Shh, girl, be quiet." *Don't make the murdering whack-a-do angry.*

By some miracle, Fluffy stopped barking. It was a fifty-fifty chance she'd obey my command at any given time. Okay, forty-sixty. Maybe thirty-seventy. I breathed a sigh of relief this was one of the times she chose to listen.

"You weren't expecting to see me, were you?"

"Um, no. The theater is closed."

"Then why are you here?" Magdalena arched one perfectly-shaped eyebrow.

I gestured to the computer and strived to keep my voice calm and steady, as though I weren't completely flipping the freak out, which in an effort for full disclosure, I have to tell you ... I was. "I needed to get some work done. What are you doing here?"

After a brief internal debate, I'd decided against mentioning the chief was on his way here. Because, if Magdalena intended to do me harm, the last thing I wanted to do was rush her into action.

"I came to see you."

"Me?" My voice squeaked. So much for calm and cool.

"Mm-hmm." She leaned one shoulder against the door frame and looked for all the world like we were in a friendly situation.

Maybe we were. I could be wrong about Magdalena being the murderer. It was possible she was here for a perfectly innocent reason.

"You see, I overheard your phone conversation on Main Street earlier." She shook her head and tsked her tongue. "You were right outside of the inn; you really should be more careful."

I licked my lips which were suddenly dry as the ground in Death Valley. Guess my hope about the friendly visit had just flown out the window. If I'd had a window in here, that is. I wished there was a window. Then I could have made a run for it by climbing out and getting away from the freakishly calm murderer who currently blocked the only way out of the office.

The calm scared me more than anything. Magdalena hadn't killed her husband in a fit of passion. It was a cold and calculated act, and the same frosty calculation shone in her eyes as she studied me from the doorway.

My only hope was if the chief got here soon. I needed to keep her talking to buy more time, either for him to arrive or for me to come up with another plan to save my own bacon.

"I didn't say anything you couldn't hear." The tightness

in my chest eased as I realized it was true. I ran my conversation with Dylan through my mind and remembered I had specifically not mentioned the murderer by name.

"You said you knew who killed Aaron."

"And you came here to ask me who did it?" I asked with a hopeful lilt to my voice.

The corners of her crimson lips tilted up, and she shook her head. "I don't need to ask you who did it, as I believe you know."

"I don't know. I don't know anything. Seriously, big empty-headed Amanda. That's what they call me."

"We both know that's not true. Your aunt has bragged about you to Pen. How smart you are, what a big career you had, how proud she is of all you've accomplished in the business world, and now you're making the leap into the world of fiction writing. Or *were* making the leap, I should say. I know you're not a ditz, so don't play games with me."

I so did not like the pointed change to the past tense when she talked about my writing career.

"You got me, I'm not empty-headed. But it doesn't mean I'm a detective." I held up my hands palms up and shrugged. "How would I know who killed Aaron?"

She stared at me through narrowed eyes for a long moment before she finally spoke. "I'm not empty-headed either. Let me tell you my interpretation of your phone call in front of the inn. Shall I?"

Continue talking to help me stall for Chief Carlow's arrival? "Yes, please."

"Based on my powers of observation, I could tell you had just come from the dismal, little salon in town. The flip-flops and the shiny, new nail polish made it obvious you'd just been for a mani/pedi. And since tiny towns like this run on gossip and judgement, I'm sure the nail technician told you about my appointment. How am I doing so far?"

"Maple Hills does like its gossip, I admit." I inclined my head. "But it's not a judgmental town. Everyone here is very welcoming and inclusive."

"Maybe, but I am right about her telling you about my appointment."

It wasn't a question, so I didn't answer.

Magdalena waited a beat and then continued, "Therefore, you know I lost one of my acrylics and made the connection to my new manicure. Maybe because you found the body, or maybe because you're seeing the police chief's yummy brother. I don't know which, but you knew about the taupe-colored acrylic fingernail found by Aaron's body. And once you knew about my emergency manicure and insistence on changing all ten nails to a dramatically different color, I knew you'd put two and two together and realized I'd killed Aaron. Because, as I said earlier, I know what an intelligent woman you are."

I'd never been so sorry to get a compliment in my life. Because if she's confessing to me about murdering her husband, I knew without a doubt I was going to be her next victim.

Chapter Eighteen

W here was Chief Carlow? I slid my hand across the desk in a surreptitious manner to reach my phone and check to see if I'd missed a call or text from him.

"Stop. Right. There."

Not surreptitiously enough, I guess. I lifted my hands in the air. "Fine."

"You don't seem to understand who is in charge here."

Oh, I understood all too well. My resolve to keep her talking strengthened, and I sent a silent wish out to the universe I was able to do so until the chief arrived. *If* the chief arrived, because there was no way of knowing if he even got my message yet.

I took a deep breath. Here goes nothing. "Why did you do it? Was it his cheating?" A thought struck me like a two-by-four, and I gasped. "Wait a minute. You don't really believe I was seeing Aaron in Los Angeles, do you? Because I wasn't. I didn't even know he existed until I started working at the theater."

She laughed, which chilled me to the bone. She was actually enjoying this situation. Playing with me, like Fluffy plays with her favorite stuffed toy. Which, for the record, is a little, purple owl.

"Trust me, I never once thought Aaron was involved with you, although you are possibly the only woman in town not sleeping with my husband. No, I just threw my accusation out there to get the police looking at someone other than me. And it worked like a charm. How many man-hours do you think they spent checking your story with your friends in LA?"

"You don't seem bothered by the infidelity," I observed.

"At one time I was. Early in our marriage. But now?" She raised one shoulder. "I was over the whole jealousy thing. It was embarrassing though, since he made no effort to hide his infidelities. I just wanted him out of my life."

"I've heard good things about divorce in that sort of situation."

"Aren't you a funny woman?" She narrowed her eyes at me. "I don't like funny women."

I swallowed hard. My throat was parched, but I didn't dare reach for the water bottle on my desk. "I'm sorry. I shouldn't have been flippant about such a serious matter."

She inhaled through her nose and huffed the breath out through her mouth. A technique I've used to calm myself in stressful situations. Good. A calm Magdalena was what I needed right now. I didn't want her to get angry and impulsive, and make her move against me too soon. I still held out hope the chief was coming. Yeah, right. So was Christmas. In six months.

"If it wasn't the cheating, why did you kill Aaron?" I was genuinely curious, and if I was going to die anyway, I wanted to get the whole story before I went.

"I'm afraid it was a very common motive." She rubbed her thumb and forefinger together. "Money, plain and simple."

"But I heard you were the one with the money in your marriage."

"I was, and I was sick of him sponging off me and using my money to run around with other women." She cocked her head. "Huh. I guess I'm not over his cheating. What do you know?"

"And insurance?" I prompted, eager to keep her talking. "I used to be in human resources, so I'm very familiar with worker's compensation insurance. As Aaron's widow, do you collect the benefits from his death while on the job? And perhaps a life insurance policy as well?"

The corners of her mouth tilted up, and she smoothed her hand over her hair. "I will get money from both of those policies as his grieving widow. A little payback for all the money he's taken from me over the years. But that's not all, as a producer of the show I stand to profit from the insurance if the show is cancelled, as well. Which it will be. Pen is trying to keep it going, but I can convince him to give it up and cancel the production."

Right, Jeremy had mentioned this type of insurance to me earlier, but I was more suspicious of Pen at that point, and hadn't seriously considered Magdalena as a suspect.

Magdalena continued, "Although the main financial incentive to me is to get him to stop spending my money. And if we divorced, he made it clear to me he would want generous spousal support from me, since most of the marital assets are mine. I should've requested a prenup, but we were so in love. I never dreamed it would come to this, so I didn't. Once the cheating started and my eyes were opened to what kind of man Aaron really was, it was too late."

"Basically money and revenge then?" I asked.

"Yes, although when you put it like that, it seems so common and trite." Magdalena pursed her lips.

I peered over her shoulder, hoping for any sign of Chief Carlow, but I couldn't see much beyond her. She was a slender woman, but tall. And the way she leaned on the doorframe, she really filled the space. My heart sank. How on earth could I get past her to make a break for it? Because I was starting to think the chief wasn't coming to my rescue. I needed to formulate my own plan to save myself. Which also required buying some time to think.

"How did you do it?" I asked, hoping against hope a narcissist like Magdalena couldn't resist the opportunity to brag about her accomplishment, criminal and horrifying as it was.

She ran her hand in the air up and down her body, like a game show hostess pointing to a prize. "You wouldn't think a woman who looked like me would know anything about stagecraft, would you? I mean, I'm so sophisticated and glamorous."

Yep, she was a narcissist all right. But it worked in my benefit, because she kept talking.

"My father taught me all about it. I spent my whole childhood in theaters, and dear old Dad was a stage manager. The best in the business. He showed me how to do everything, and in an old hemp house theater like this one. It was ridiculously easy for me to manipulate the rope to give way." She frowned and stared a point over my head. "I thought everyone would think it was an accident. I was careful to make the rope look frayed, not cut."

"But Chief Carlow realized," I said.

She wagged her finger at me. "He did. He's smarter than I expected. I thought a yokel cop in a backwater town like this one would just accept the obvious solution and get back to eating his apple cider donuts."

"What I don't understand is how you got Aaron to stand in just the right place on the stage?"

"It was genius." She clasped her hands together. "The crew was struggling with the rigging system, since they're all used to a more modern setup, but Aaron knew I had experience in hemp houses. He'd complained the lighting on Maisy wasn't right for one of her numbers. I offered to come in early, before rehearsal, and position the light properly for him."

I snapped my fingers. "That's why you were dressed the way you were. You weren't walking in the woods, you were scrambling around in the rigging."

She tapped one long, blood red fingernail to her nose. "Bing, bing, bing. Give the little lady a prize."

All right, I needed to get her mind off that idea, because I suspected her idea of a prize and my idea of a prize were not at all the same thing. Hers would be much more fatal to me.

"Did you come here planning to kill Aaron with the light? How could you have known about the lighting issues?"

"Pen had been keeping me updated on the situation here. He said it was a debacle, and he wished my dad were still alive to take this crew in hand and teach them the ropes. Literally." Her laughter tinkled like crystal at her own joke.

"So this was your plan all along?"

"It was. Clever, no?"

"Extremely." Diabolical was really the word I would use, but no sense in antagonizing the crazy lady who already wants to kill me. "And you couldn't risk just leaving the rope ready to give, because it might fall on anyone, or no one. You had to get Aaron into place and do your thing with the rope at just the right moment."

"You're smart. I like you. It's a shame I have to kill you."

~

"You really don't have to. I can keep a secret. Being discrete is part of the deal when you're in human resources. I knew all kinds of personal things about employees I couldn't share." I mimed zipping my lips.

"Oh, but I do. Like I said, I don't really want to kill you, but you know too much. And you're dating the police chief's brother, so there's no way you could keep my secret." She shuddered. "Plus you seem all honorable."

How did she make it seem like an insult? "Thank you, I think."

"It wasn't a compliment. I prefer people who will do whatever needs to be done to achieve their goals, no matter what. Like I do."

I glanced at Fluffy, but the deceptively civil tone of Magdalena and my interaction had lulled her into a false sense of security, and she dozed on her dog bed. For once, I wouldn't mind if my girl went all Beast on someone, but no such luck. I was thinking it would have to be a team effort between Fluffy and me, if we were going to make it out of this tiny, dark office alive. I cleared my throat loudly to awaken the sleeping Beast ... I mean, Fluffy.

She lifted her head and blinked at me sleepily. My plan wasn't totally formulated yet, I needed a little more time to mull.

Much as I hated to broach this particular topic, I asked Magdalena, "How do you plan to kill me? You can't drop a light on my head.'

"Why not?"

"For one thing, you'd have to wrestle me out to the stage, and I don't want to die. I wouldn't make it easy for you. And for another thing, there's no way anyone would think for a moment it was an accident. They would know it was murder."

"And there's the greater problem. I have my means to force you to the stage, if I really wanted you to go there, but it can't look like murder."

I swiped my sweaty palms on my shorts. Her words did not sound good at all. Did she have a concealed weapon?

She smiled at my obvious discomfort. The woman was enjoying the lead-up to my murder a little too much.

"Plus you've tried to kill me that way already, didn't you? The light almost falling on me was no accident."

She stuck her chest out and practically purred like a cat with a bowl of cream. "No, it wasn't. I did that too. Your annoying dog saved your skin that day. She won't now." She shook her head as if to clear it. "But back to today. You're right, the falling light is so yesterday. It's why I have a different plan. I made it up on the fly, after I overheard your phone call. I'm rather proud of myself." She pulled a small vial out of her pocket, and displayed it between her thumb and forefinger. "I'm going to poison you."

"Poison? Why did you have poison with you?" My voice squeaked, and my increasing panic must have been palpable to Fluffy because she no longer looked sleepy. She was wide awake and alert, looking between Magdalena and me.

"It was my Plan B with Aaron, in case the lighting thing didn't work. I was going to poison his morning coffee."

"It's good to have a back-up plan," I said. But I wasn't thinking of hers, so much as mine in case the chief didn't appear soon. Like, really soon. Now, would be nice. "But I would still be obviously murdered. How do you think you're going to get away with it?'

Because there wasn't any doubt this very organized

killer had her end-game planned out to the last detail. I could almost admire it, if I wasn't in total fear for my life.

"I'm going to make it look like suicide."

Her tone was threatening enough, Fluffy stood and growled low in her throat. She frowned at my dog, and added, "Maybe I'll even kill your little dog, too and make it look like you did it."

"Okay, wicked witch, why would I kill Fluffy? Everyone knows I adore my dog." I kept my tone flippant, but my heart raced at the notion she would hurt Fluffy too.

She tapped a crimson nail on her chin. "You do love the little mutt." Her eyes opened wide, and she grinned. "But no one else does, and you're afraid no one will care for her after you're gone, so you kill her first and then kill yourself. It's touching, in its own way."

"It still will look like murder, because I'm not the least bit suicidal, and everyone knows it."

"Ah, but you're going to type a suicide note on your laptop for me. When they find your bodies, everyone will see the note right away."

"Why would I type a suicide note for you? With all due respect for your plan, because being an organized woman myself, and I do appreciate a well-thought-out plan, there's no way I'm just going to type out the note for you."

She pulled a gun out of her purse. She was prepared for every kind of murder in that handbag. Poison, guns, what would emerge next from it? A machete?

"Because the alternative to you not typing the note is I shoot your dog in front of you, and then kill you."

"Not to be repetitive or anything, but that would still obviously be murder."

She waved her gun at her purse. " Then I'll amend the note to say you've shot yourself and the dog. I've got gloves in here. I can always type your faux suicide note myself, without leaving fingerprints. But I'd prefer to make you do it."

I crinkled my nose. "Why?"

"Because it's more fun for me. Now type what I dictate."

"No." I rose from my chair.

Her eyebrows lifted, and her scarlet lips formed a perfect 'O'. "No? What do you mean *no*?" She waved her gun at my chair. "Sit yourself back down, and type what I tell you to."

"I. Said. No." I took a step toward Fluffy, and Magdalena swung the gun between the two of us.

"What are you doing? I've got a gun."

And I had a plan. A reckless plan, possibly doomed to failure, but I had to try something. Without preamble, I shouted, "Get her, Fluffy."

In the blink of an eye, Fluffy charged at Magdalena, barking furiously. I was hot on her tail, and I roared like a lion as I charged the woman.

The element of surprise worked in our favor, as if Magdalena had never expected any resistance. She stood rooted in place, with her jaw dropped and the gun held slack in her hand.

I didn't pause before I ran right into her, pushing as hard as I could. She staggered, and it moved her just enough to give me space to squeeze past her into the lobby.

Unfortunately, she didn't stay frozen by surprise for long, and dove after me. She caught me by my shoulder, and I stumbled, but she did too. Wait, why did she stumble too?

Fluffy's menacing growl reached my ears. It sounded just like when we played tug-of-war with her little owl. I looked down and saw her teeth bared where they gripped the bottom of Magdalena's stylish maxi-dress. Fluffy shook her head back and forth rapidly, and I heard the sound of fabric ripping.

"You stupid little rat. This is a designer dress. It's silk, and you're ruining it!" Magdalena shrieked at Fluffy and swatted at her with her gun.

Better swatting than shooting. And I knew from playing with Fluffy, she was excellent at the tuggy game. Her jaws were like a steel trap. She'd never let go.

Still, seeing my beloved little companion in danger infuriated me. I'd bottle fed Fluffy when she was a newborn puppy, abandoned at the shelter. I fought to keep her alive then and

was not about to let her life end this way.

"Don't hurt my dog," I shouted as I reached out and yanked Magdalena's hair. Hard.

She winced, and her head pulled back on her neck. "That hurts."

"Good," I said as I pulled back my fist. "This will hurt more."

There was a burst of satisfaction at the crunching sound when my fist made contact with her nose. My hand throbbed, and I waved it in the air.

She swiped at the blood coming out of her nose. "What is wrong with you? I have a gun."

"Drop the weapon, Mrs. Hillner." Chief Carlow stepped through the open doorway into the theater, with his own gun drawn and aimed directly at Magdalena.

"Thank goodness you're here. This woman and her dog are attacking me. Please help me, officer." She batted her long, false eyelashes at Danny.

Huh. All it took for me to start thinking of the chief as Danny was him helping to save Fluffy and my lives.

"That's *Chief* Carlow. And unfortunately for you, I heard the whole thing, Mrs. Hillner. You are clearly the aggressor here. Now drop the gun. I'm placing you under arrest for the murder of your husband, and the attempted murder of Amanda Seldon."

She paused, and for a split second I feared she'd kill Danny and me both, but finally with a resigned sigh, Magdalena held out her gun to Danny.

Too wrapped up in her attack/game, Fluffy still tugged at her dress. I tapped my thigh. "Game's over, Fluff. Come here."

Fluffy released the dress and trotted over to my side. I picked her up and held her close. Now the threat was over, all the blood drained from my head to my feet as I fully realized just how close we'd come to death.

My voice was shaky when I spoke. "Good girl, Fluff. You helped save my life. Again."

Danny turned Magdalena so her back was to him and snapped on the cuffs. He beamed over at me. "You saved each other's lives. Nice work, Seldon. You really are good enough for my brother."

Chapter Nineteen

"Have you put her down since you picked her up at the theater this afternoon?" Danny gestured with his beer bottle to Fluffy.

She was perched on my lap, as I sat in an Adirondack chair by the pond in Dylan's backyard. "Only briefly." I admitted. "Once it was all over and you had Magdalena in handcuffs, reality came crashing down on me. While everything was happening with Magdalena, I had to keep my cool. But when it was over, I got a little shaky. I'm holding on to her as much for me, as for Fluffy."

The corners of his eyes crinkled as he smiled down at me. "A delayed reaction to a stressful situation. I see it happen all the time in my line of work. But you did good back there. You kept your head and saved your life. You saved each other's lives." He reached down to scratch Fluffy's head, and she bared her teeth. He snatched back his hand. "She is a ferocious little thing."

"Thank goodness she can be, and thank you."

Jeremy and Cara walked over to us. Jeremy handed me a glass of rosé, and Cara sat in the Adirondack chair next to mine. I savored a sip of the crisp, dry wine, and resisted the urge to down the whole thing in one swig. It had been a day.

"Hey, Danny. Nice of your brother to have us all over for a cookout tonight. Everyone wanted to see for themselves Amanda was safe and sound. I know I did."

"Me too. After Jeremy told me what happened, I had my parents call me as soon as Amanda got home and raced over to her house to see her with my own eyes." Cara stretched out her hand and clasped mine briefly. It was the hand I'd used to punch Magdalena, so the contact hurt a little, but it was worth it.

"What's going to happen to Magdalena now?" Jeremy asked.

Danny took a sip of his beer and shrugged. "She lawyered up right away, so we couldn't talk to her, but I heard her whole confession at the theater before Amanda and Fluffy took her down."

I narrowed my eyes at him. "About that. You really could've let me know you were there sooner."

"If I had, you might've given it away, and I wanted to hear the full confession. Nice work getting her to talk, by the way."

"Once I realized her ego was the size of Brazil, it was easy to get her to brag about her crimes. She was only too eager to tell me how clever she'd been."

My mouth watered as the wind shifted and carried the scent of grilling burgers through the air. Fluffy raised her head and sniffed. Dylan had been manning the grill for a while, but I glanced in that direction and saw Jeremy's husband Eric had taken over and Dylan was strolling my way with a plate in his hand.

"I bet you haven't eaten since breakfast," he said as he handed me the plate.

My stomach growled so loudly Fluffy whipped her head around to look at my belly. Heat raced into my cheeks. "It seems I am hungry."

"Eric told me how you like your burgers."

"Pickles, ketchup, and mustard?"

"Yep. And a slice of cheddar. Dig in," Dylan said.

I complied eagerly. I was too hungry to let good manners get in the way, and worry about the fact no one else had any food.

"I think I'm going to head over to the grill and grab me a hot dog," Danny said.

Cara rose. "Take my chair, Dylan. We'll go too."

"We will?" Jeremy asked.

She widened her eyes and gestured pointedly with her head from Dylan to me and back again. "Yes, we will."

Jeremy started. "Right, yeah, we will. Talk to you later." He leaned down and pressed a brief kiss to the top of my head. "I'm glad you're not dead."

"Yeah, being dead would really suck. Especially right after I moved home."

"I know, right?" Jeremy winked at me before following Cara to the patio where the built-in grill was.

Dylan gazed at me as I inhaled another bite of my burger. I swiped at my chin. "What? Do I have mustard on my face?"

"No, I'm just enjoying looking at you. When Danny called to tell me what happened, I was out of my head. We just found each other, after all these years, and I almost lost you. The only thing stopping me from charging down to the police station right away was the fact you were in the middle of giving your statement."

"You were there when I came out of the interview room though." I slanted him a glance, before taking another bite of burger.

"Oh, I still charged to the station house, but not right away. I finished what I was doing, and texted Jeremy first." His cheeks grew ruddy.

I swallowed and reached out one hand to hold his, where it rested on the arm of the chair. He glanced at my red, puffy knuckles, before gently taking it into his own.

"I was really happy to see you when I walked out of the interview room."

Now it was my turn to blush, based on the heat which flooded my cheeks. I remembered the way I raced to him when I emerged after giving my statement, and how Dylan had embraced both Fluffy and me, since I couldn't bring myself to put her down yet. In spite of a little canine obstacle, he'd managed to get close enough to give me a passionate kiss in front of most of the Maple Hills Police Department. Oh, and Jeremy, who'd skidded in to the police station while Dylan was kissing me.

I finished my burger and wadded up the napkin and plopped it on my plate, and put both on the ground. Time for a change of subject, before my face actually caught fire from embarrassment. "Your house looks terrific."

"Thanks. I did a lot of remodeling after my parents retired and moved away. With their blessing. They said they'd made it their own when my grandparents passed, and it was my turn to make it my own."

Aunt Lori rushed up to us, with Pen Adams by her side.

"We just got here. How are you, Mandy-bel?" She held her arms open wide. I put Fluffy down, stood up, and stepped into her embrace.

"I'm okay." My voice was muffled from the fact my face was pressed into her shoulder.

Pen swung his head slowly from side to side. "I still can't believe Magdalena killed Aaron."

"And almost Amanda and Fluffy too." She released me

from her tight hug. "Sit back down, Mandy-bel. You should rest."

"I'm not sick, Aunt Lori." *Just almost murdered.*

Fluffy nudged my ankle with her wet nose, and I got the hint and picked her up and took Aunt Lori's advice and sat back down with Fluffy on my lap. I ran my hands over the velvety fur on her back.

Jeremy and Cara trotted back to us.

"Since Lori and Pen interrupted your moment with each other, we figured it was safe to come back," Jeremy said.

Cara smacked him on the arm. "Smooth. Not."

"I'm sorry if we interrupted a personal moment, I just wanted to tell you I'm going back to New York in the morning," Pen said.

"You are? What about the show?" Jeremy asked.

"I decided to cancel production. It seems doomed. And without either my coproducer or my director, I don't really have the heart for it."

My heart ached for Pen who suddenly looked his age. "I'm sorry. Aunt Lori told me you've known Magdalena since she was a child. It must be very difficult for you."

"It is. I remember when she was born. I'm even her godfather." He inhaled deeply and gazed out over the pond. "For the first time since they both passed, I'm glad her parents aren't here. This would've broken both of their hearts."

We all sat in silence for a moment, as the sun set over the green hills in the distance.

Pen turned to Jeremy and extended his hand. "Obviously, I'll pay for the use of the theater for the entire run, even though we won't be using it."

Jeremy shook hands with him. "Thank you. The owner will be relieved to hear it."

"I won't intrude on your evening any longer. Good night."

"I'll walk you to your car," Aunt Lori said.

Cara watched them with avid interest. "Do you think they're going to see each other again?"

"Maybe. Casually, but it's nothing serious. And I have it on firm authority, straight from the horse's mouth."

"Ooo ... did you just call Lori a horse? I'm telling." Jeremy chortled.

"What are you, twelve?" Cara asked.

I beamed at both of them while they bickered in the way only lifelong friends could.

"What are you smiling at?" Dylan asked.

"It's good to be home," I replied.

"It's good to have you home." He took my hand and held it.

The setting sun caused the pond to glow a fiery orange. I sighed. "I'd forgotten just how beautiful it is here."

"In the summer. Talk to me again when you're having to shovel your car out of a foot of snow," Cara said.

"You can't beat this part of the world in the fall, though," Jeremy said.

"I never really get to enjoy it," Dylan grimaced. "Fall is our busy season. Working dawn 'til dusk once the leaf-peepers descend on Maple Hills. But I can't complain, their love of apple cider and our maple sugar candy pays the bills."

"Amanda will be out of work again in the fall, maybe she can help out with the orchard?" Jeremy suggested.

"Thanks for being my manager, Jeremy, but Dylan and I have already discussed it."

"And if Amanda wants a job, she's got one here," Dylan said.

"The theater closes after Labor Day, and then I will

need another job. But part-time only. I need time to write, and I haven't gotten as much done as I planned so far."

"You've been busy taking down a murderer. Give yourself a break," Cara said.

"True." I bobbed my head.

Jeremy lifted his beer bottle in a toast. "To the first scene of Amanda Seldon's Second Act. It's been a doozy."

I raised my wine glass and took a sip. "It sure has been. But now things can calm down and Maple Hills will go back to being its usual sleepy, peaceful, murder-free self."

You know what they say about tempting fate? In retrospect, I realized I'd thrown down the gauntlet to fate, and fate had taken it up with a vengeance. But in the moment, I basked in the happiness of having a beautiful sunset to savor and a delicious glass of wine in my hand. Not to mention my two best friends with me and the unexpected pleasure of Dylan by my side. It seemed impossible to believe more murder was coming our way. But it was.

DID YOU ENJOY AMANDA AND FLUFFY'S ESCAPADES? IF SO, please consider leaving a review on your favorite site.

Their story continues in book two of the Second Act Cozy Mystery series, **An Apple a Slay.** Coming soon!

IN THE MEANTIME, TRY A VISIT TO PORT SUNSET, FLORIDA. A Gulf Coast town inhabited by fun-loving, quirky residents, but with an unfortunate body count. Take a peek at book one in my Port Sunset Cozy Mystery series, **Penthouse, Pools, and Poison** ...

.   .   .

"ANOTHER CRISIS AVERTED. THANKS TO YOU, ELLIS." I slurped the last of my iced hazelnut coffee through the straw in the to-go cup and leaned against the padded wall of the hotel's service elevator.

The weathered face of the Gulf Palms Resort and Spa's maintenance man creased as he grinned at me. Ellis Smith was a notorious curmudgeon, and his smiles were as rare as snow in Port Sunset, Florida. But, for some reason, he'd always had a soft spot for me, and I'm super fond of the older man too—like an honorary uncle. The crazy uncle no one ever talks about in company, but my favorite, nonetheless.

"No problem, Millie. I'm just glad they noticed the leaky pipe in the backroom of the gift shop before it caused any real damage." His deep voice rumbled, and I heard the hint of a northern accent, in spite of all the decades he'd lived here in Port Sunset, Florida. A refugee from Connecticut winters myself, I recognized the slight accent as possibly being from northern New England.

His background was a mystery. Ellis did not like to talk about the past. He didn't like to talk much, period. He liked me better than anyone else at the hotel, and even I couldn't get him to open up to me.

The elevator binged right before the doors slid open. Ellis held the door back from automatically closing with one hand, and gestured for me to get out before him with the other. I flashed him a grin as I scooted out of the elevator into the grand, marble lobby of the Gulf Palms. Stan the bellman waited outside the service elevator, with a rolling luggage cart filled to overflowing, and Ellis held up his hand like a traffic cop and growled at Stan to keep him from pushing ahead of me to board the elevator. Seriously. Ellis growled. Like I said, he liked me better than anyone else at the hotel.

Stan fought against a grin and lost. As I stepped up next to him, he said out of the corner of his mouth, "What's your secret with Ellis? You're the only one he treats like a human being."

I shrugged. "Must be my natural charm."

To be honest, I think it was because I talked to Ellis when I first started working here. I didn't know he had a reputation for keeping to himself. Okay, keeping to himself is an understatement. He had a reputation for being a complete and total crabby hermit. I just talked to him like I would anyone else, and he didn't rebuff me the way he did other people, and over time we became good friends.

Stan laughed, but lingered in the lobby, as the elevator doors closed.

The gleaming marble lobby was blindingly white, and the windows looking over the Gulf of Mexico let in all the bright Florida sunshine. The lobby was decorated in the hotel's trademark pink and green, just like my work uniform capri pants, which were pink with little green palm trees embroidered on them. The Gulf Palms Resort managed to walk the line between comfortably welcoming and grand. Usually music played quietly in the lobby, either piped in over the sound system, or performed by a pianist at the grand piano tucked away in a corner by the Swaying Palms Bar. However, right now, the sounds reaching my ears were a lot less melodic.

"I thought the Gulf Palms Resort was supposed to be a class place, not some rinky-dink operation!" The man's face was red as a beet, as he yelled at the young woman behind the check-in desk.

"Who's the heart attack waiting to happen?" I whispered out of the corner of my mouth to Stan, as he leaned around me and pressed the call button for the elevator again.

"Eugene Tarkington. His family checked in last night after you left. I was just watching the show, but I better get these bags up to their owners." He winked at me as he rolled the cart onto the service elevator. "Let me know how it turns out."

I took one last bracing sip of my iced coffee, and tossed the empty to-go cup into the trash next to the elevator, as the doors slid shut on Stan. I frowned at the scene before me. The woman working the desk this morning was little more than a kid, a college student, who worked here part-time. What kind of bully would be talking to her this way?

"I better go help Emily," I said in a low voice to Ellis, who stared at the sight in the lobby through eyes fit to bug out of his head.

He cleared his throat, and his voice was gravely and low when he replied, "Good luck. You're gonna need it."

"Thanks." I crinkled my nose as I peered at Ellis. He normally ignored the guests as much as possible, and as a result, was never rattled by this type of outburst. I wondered what was up with him, but couldn't take the time to get to the bottom of the mystery right now. Usually, I loved my work in this beautiful tropical resort, but in this moment I wished I was anywhere else. I forced a smile as bright and cheerful as the lobby to my face as I approached the angry man. I knew the moment Emily spotted me, because her face brightened, in spite of the tears glistening in her eyes.

"May I be of assistance?" I asked in what I hoped was a cheerful tone, but the truth was I was angry enough to pop this guy in the nose for making Emily cry.

"Who the hell are you?" The man hollered. He was a big man, but soft looking. I knew the type all-too-well from working here. Rich, used to getting everything he wants, and unwelcome as a gator on a golf course.

"My name is Millie Wentworth, and I'm the Assistant General Manager of the Gulf Palms. What seems to be the problem, sir?"

"I don't deal with assistants. Where's the general manager?" The man demanded, looking over my head as he asked, as if expecting the general manager to appear out of thin air at his command.

"Mr. Clark is off the premises at the moment, but why don't you let me know what's happening, and perhaps I can help you."

Little did the big loudmouth know, even if the GM, Vincent Clark, was here, he'd be hiding in his office right now, after delegating me to deal with the angry guest. Confrontation was not Vince's jam. My nickname around the resort was 'the Fixer', and I took pride in the fact there wasn't a discontented guest I couldn't soothe. At least up until now there wasn't.

The man huffed. "Fine. I'm Eugene Tarkington."

He paused at this point, as if he expected me to genuflect at the sound of his name.

"Nice to meet you, Mr. Tarkington," I replied, my professional smile still firmly in place, in spite of the fact I was sticking imaginary pins into my imaginary voodoo doll of Eugene.

The crimson red in his cheeks, had died down to a more subdued shade, but he was still clearly cheesed off. He jerked his thumb at a very attractive, younger woman behind him. Maybe his daughter?

"My wife—"

Nope. Not his daughter. A trophy wife. She was lovely, tall and statuesque, with perfectly coiffed and highlighted hair. She looked slightly bored with the scene before her, and she barely acknowledged my presence with a faint nod of her head, before she went back to inspecting her long fingernails.

"—wanted a manicure and pedicure at the spa this afternoon, and when she called down, she was told there were no appointments available until tomorrow." His voice rose, until the end of the sentence was back to the ear-splitting volume it had been when I'd arrived on the scene.

"I'm very sorry, Mr. Tarkington—"

"Sorry?!" He interrupted me with a bellow, and his face was back to mid-summer, beefsteak tomato red again. He pointed at Emily behind the desk. "This one was sorry too. What good does sorry do? Sorry won't get my wife's nails done."

My smile faltered a bit, but I tried to keep my tone of voice upbeat and cheerful. "Let me call the Tranquility Spa, and see what I can do. Would you care for a glass of champagne while I do so?"

Before her husband could start yelling again, Mrs. Tarkington perked up at the magic word 'champagne', and said, "I would."

"Not for me, I'm more of a Scotch man," Mr. Tarkington said.

I smiled at the young woman behind the desk, "Emily, please get Mrs. Tarkington a glass of champagne, and Mr. Tarkington our finest Scotch from the bar." I turned to look at the problem guest, who looked somewhat appeased at this point. "If you'd wait here, I'm just going to nip behind the desk to my office and call the spa manager to get things straightened out for you."

"That's more like it. Action. That's what I expect from subordinates when I have a problem. Oh! And one more thing—the toilet in the master bedroom is running, not up to my standards, missie."

Mrs. Tarkington appeared to roll her eyes, but it was done so quickly, I couldn't be sure.

"Luckily for you, I happen to be with the best maintenance man in the business, and he can take care of your plumbing issue in no time." I flashed a cocky grin and jerked my thumb over my shoulder at Ellis.

Mr. Tarkington craned his head to look behind me and scowled. "I don't see anybody."

I turned to look and Ellis had vanished. Huh. Maybe the yelling stressed him out more than I'd realized. I wondered if Ellis suffered from PTSD. I frowned, and pulled my smartphone out of the pocket of my capri pants. "He must have had another matter to attend to. I'll text him, and ask him to get to the penthouse ASAP."

Tarkington grunted in response. What lovely manners. The old saying that money can't buy class, sprung to my mind. I wonder why?

As I hurried to a door just past the check-in desk that led to the management offices, I tapped out a quick text with my thumbs, asking Ellis to fix the running toilet as soon as he could. I held up a key card on my key chain, and opened the door after it beeped. I entered the second office on the left, which was mine. My boss scored the coveted big office behind the first door and a small conference room was at the end of the hall. I tossed my purse onto the desk, and didn't bother to turn on the lights, or even to sit down, as I suspected Mr. Tarkington was not a patient man. I hit the speed dial button on my desktop phone to reach the spa.

"Hi, it's Millie. I need Maria, stat. We have a defcon level angry guest whose wife wants a mani/pedi."

After being on hold for a few seconds, I heard the Cuban accented voice of Maria Garcia, the spa manager. "Let me guess...the Tarkingtons?"

"You're psychic, Maria. They made poor Emily cry. I'm plying them with expensive booze right now, what can you do for me?"

"Give me five minutes to see what I can do, and then bring her over. I'll do her stinking nails myself if I have to."

"I owe you."

"Yes. Yes you do," Maria said, but I could hear the smile in her voice.

"See you in five," I said before I hung up the desk phone.

~

"MR. TARKINGTON, WE'LL HAVE SOMEONE FROM maintenance up to fix the running toilet at the earliest possible opportunity," I said with an admittedly phony, cheery smile.

"I should hope so," he blustered in return. Although, the glass of fine scotch he held seemed to have ratcheted down his anger a bit.

I turned my head to speak to the sullen looking Mrs. Tarkington. "And, if you'll please come with me, Mrs. Tarkington, we can head over to the Tranquility Spa. The manager is arranging things for you as we speak."

Mrs. Tarkington inclined her head in a regal manner, but with the air of a woman who was used to people jumping through hoops to give her what she wanted. "Thank you, Millie."

Her husband squinted at me over his crystal rocks glass. "Millie is a funny name for a young woman. It makes you sound like an old broad."

"I go by Millie, but I was named after my paternal grandmother, Mildred Wentworth," I replied, although my smile faltered around the edges a bit by this point. I turned back to Mrs. Tarkington and said, "You may bring your champagne with you." I swept my hand out to the far end of the lobby, "The spa entrance is on the left up ahead. After you."

"I'm going back up to sit by the private pool on our rooftop deck," Mr. Tarkington hollered after us. "Don't know why all of the kids are at the public pool and beach with the hoi polloi."

His wife shrugged with complete and total disinterest and walked ahead of me towards the spa. She called over her shoulder, "I'll be back later. I might try to get a massage too, while I'm at the spa."

I flashed Mr. Tarkington one final smile, and scrambled to catch up with Mrs. Tarkington. The woman had to be almost six feet tall, and all legs. Even though her movements were languid, she was covering some serious distance with each step. At five foot six, I consider myself average height, but she towered over me. I wondered if she'd been a model when she met her husband. She had the look of one. I tugged self-consciously at my ponytail. I'd been running late this morning, and just pulled my brown hair back to save time, rather than styling it. I hoped I didn't look too much of a mess, although compared to Mrs. Tarkington, there weren't many women who wouldn't look a little frumpy.

"I think Millie is a sweet name," she said.

"Thank you," My eyes widened in surprise, at her words. They were the most she'd said so far, and were almost...kind. Not at all what I expected to hear from her.

"My husband doesn't always realize how he sounds, and people might take offense where none was intended. Like the 'old broad' comment before."

"No worries. He's right, it is kind of an old-fashioned name. My other grandmother is called Lulu."

Mrs. Tarkington smiled, and her appearance was transformed. She was truly lovely. "I think I'd be glad I was named Millie, after my other grandmother, in that case."

I raised one shoulder in a shrug, and warmth spread in the general vicinity of my heart at the thought of my beloved grandmother. "Lulu suits her. She's a real pip."

We reached the salon, and I held the door open for Mrs. Tarkington. I followed her into the spa lobby, where we were greeted by the soothing scent of lavender, and mellow, instrumental spa music. The sort of plinky-plinky New Age music they always played in spas.

A young, dark-skinned woman was at the front desk. Her hair was in long braids, which were tied back in a ponytail, and she wore the spa version of the Gulf Palms staff uniform. A tunic style jacket, with leggings, both in the trademark pink, with tiny, green palm trees on them. A sage green, and subdued pale pink, were the predominate colors of the spa's décor, and a large potted palm was in the center of the lobby area. Products available for sale were discreetly displayed on shelves built into the walls.

"Hello, Millie," the young woman greeted me, with a Caribbean lilt to her voice.

"Hiya, Tanya. This is—"

"Mrs. Tarkington," Another woman spoke as she entered from a glass door behind the front desk, which led to the salon. The petite, middle-aged woman came out from behind the desk, with her hand extended in greeting. She had dark hair pulled back in a bun, and spoke with a slight Cuban accent, "I'm Maria Garcia, the manager of Tranquility Spa and Salon. Welcome."

"Hello," Mrs. Tarkington answered, and held out her hand to limply and very briefly shake Maria's.

"I'm very sorry for any confusion about your appointment today." Maria gestured to a door on the other side of the front desk, just past the comfy seats in the waiting area. "The dressing rooms are through there. Tanya, please take Mrs. Tarkington, and let her change into a robe for her treatments." While she spoke, she removed the empty champagne flute from Mrs. Tarkington's hand. "Let me take care of that for you, ma'am. We'll have another glass waiting for you at your manicure station."

"Thank you," Mrs. Tarkington said, as she followed Tanya to the door. At the last moment, she turned and spoke as if it were an afterthought, "And thank you for your help with our problems today, Millie."

"You are very welcome," I said to the woman's back as she walked through the door, which closed with a thunk behind her, while I was still speaking.

Maria rolled her eyes, and spoke in a soft voice, "She's charming."

"Compared to her husband, she is," I whispered back, with a dramatic eye roll.

"Lulu was in this morning for a mani/pedi. Evidently, she has a hot date tonight."

I heaved a sigh. "It's a sad state of affairs, when my seventy-something grandmother has a more active social life than I do."

"You need to get out of this place more often. You work too hard," Maria waved the empty champagne glass at me.

"You're a fine one to talk. When's the last time you had a day off, huh?"

"Point taken," Maria said, "Hey, Lulu and her crew are by the pool. Why don't you take a break and head out to see her?"

"Good idea. I think I will. I want to find out who this hot date is with tonight."

$\sim$

To keep reading, download **PENTHOUSE, POOLS, & Poison** today.

And check out the rest of the Port Sunset series too, **Diamonds, Dunes, & Death**, **Sunshine, Selfies, & Smugglers**, and **Cabanas, Cupids, & Corpses**.

Acknowledgments

Most of the time, writing involves sitting alone while my fictional characters have adventures in my head, which I then transcribe to the page. And then endlessly, edit, revise, and tweak it until I finally throw up my hands and announce, "I'm done!"

But I do also get a lot of help and support from my friends and family. For this book, I really appreciated my dear friend Kenneth Lockie taking the time to meet with me and talk about his human resources career. It helped me tremendously in fleshing out Amanda's history and her character.

Also thanks to my sister Mary for reading the rough first chapter, to help me be sure Amanda had her own voice and wasn't just 'Millie goes to New England'. Also, my fabulous author friend, Claire Marti, always beta reads for me and helps me make my work better every single time. And in addition to all his other support, Leo also read through this one. Twice. And gave me valuable input.

Huge thanks to Elizabeth Mackey for another amazing cover design, Trish Long for her expert copy editing, and Shasta Schafer for her thorough proofreading. It's a pleasure to work with you ladies!

Last, but most definitely not least, thank you to all my readers! It means so much to me every time you read my books, leave a review, or let me know on social media that you enjoy my work. It keeps me going!

About the Author

Louise Stevens is the author of the Port Sunset Mysteries, and the Second Act Cozy Mystery series. A lover of mysteries since her discovery of Nancy Drew many years ago, she is thrilled to be writing cozy mysteries now. She lives in Maryland with her husband, who also loves a good mystery, in a house packed with books.

Louise Stevens is the pen name of contemporary romance author Donna Simonetta.

Made in United States
Cleveland, OH
21 April 2025

16269259R00132